Introductions

...a story about God

Introductions

...a story about God

Matthew D. Harding

*hybris think tank
publishing*

PUBLISHED BY HYBRIS THINK TANK
11404 E. Renata Ave, Suite 1, Mesa, AZ 85212

www.hybristhinktank.com

Printed in the United States of America
First Printing: July 2010

Library of Congress Cataloging-in-Publication Data is available

ISBN 978-0-9842663-0-2

Everyone is trying to put together their own puzzle with shades of gray where it contacts others. Everyone has special attributes that they must discover and then fully develop. Writing this book took me on the most amazing adventure that resulted in a truer understanding of "how to be" as well as helped me connect some more of my own pieces.

I hope this book will help anyone brave enough to look for the answers inside, find enlightenment, peace, and the reality of truth.

-Matthew D. Harding

Any intelligent fool can make things

bigger, more complex, and more violent.

It takes a touch of genius - and a lot of

courage –

to move in the opposite direction.

Albert Einstein

Introductions

...a story about God

What if He is real?

What if...

there is something absolutely vital inside for you to

read?

Would you find it?

CHAPTER ONE

Sky Harbor airport
Phoenix, Arizona
July 26, 2009

Phoenix in July.

Nothing quite like that 115 degrees of scorching dry heat beating down on you as you walk as quickly as you can from one air-conditioned building to the next. Oh, but it's a dry heat they say....what does that mean? Nothing dry about 115 degrees because if you are moving it still leaves you drenched in your own sweat!

Standing there, hot - my head slightly crooked staring at the sign that told me I was right where I needed to be yet I had no idea how my day would unfold.

Tuning out all the sadness and animosity of the world around me, I closed my eyes and turned inward for the familiar presence of Me and the comfort and contentment I feel about my life, my world, and who I am.

I am happy.

Not just a statement but a truth.

Refocused, I took a deep breath and returned to the chaos of thousands of people trying to get where they need to go, all attempting to be on time, to be pseudo accurate in their life, most are rushing through this airport, on this day, just as unsure about how their day would unfold as I was. But I knew I was right where I was supposed to be.

I looked up again at the sign that read Gate B-8.

I had arrived at my first destination of the day, the one that would take me to my next.

A seat in the middle of the lobby for B-8 caught my eye. The seat was placed perfectly between an older, grey haired gentleman and an impeccably beautiful woman with dusty blond hair. I was instantly drawn to the situation, as it was the only seat in the terminal that was currently unoccupied.

I began the trek to take my soon-to-be seat, checking my phone for the time as I walked, *sure enough, more than two hours until my flight would even begin to board*, I thought, *might as well get comfortable.*

As I made my way to the lone seat available in B-8, I noticed a book sitting right in the center of my promising seat. I had to consider if it was a marker to save the seat and if so, what I would do about it. As I got closer I noticed that the book, itself, was beautiful, not the kind of book someone would just leave carelessly in an airport.

I picked the book up slowly...initially, for dramatic reasons but I was also a bit drawn to the unique, simple nature of the book; I was hoping I wouldn't hear someone say, "that's my book". Something about the book looked... just plain cool, and old, like an antique, something that had been in the "family" for a long time. I was somewhat interested in checking it out.

It is probably the gray haired guy's book and he is just trying to keep someone from sitting next to him.

I cast a quick glance around to see if anyone was going to lay claim to this remarkable yet simple book but there was not a word from the crowd.

I cleared my throat slightly, dramatically, to have someone, anyone, respond if it was their book, otherwise I was going to pick it up, sit down and keep it.

Still nothing from the multitude surrounding me...

There are two obvious suspects as to the owners of this particular book. The first is the grey haired man to my right, although he seems lost in a crossword puzzle, oblivious to the world around him. The second suspect is this beautiful, blond woman engrossed in a magazine with her blackberry in her lap.

Even so, I must break both their concentrations.

"Excuse me sir, but does this book belong to you?"

He stared at me for a moment in a way that made me reconsider his ability to fully process my question, as if he knew an answer but to a different question.

He replied, almost roughly, "Not mine," and immediately returned to his crossword puzzle.

So… I guess the book is not his. Well one down, one to go.

I slowly rolled my head to my left, to the blond, thinking, that if this book belonged to anybody around me that by now someone watching would certainly have spoken up.

I was instantly looking into her eyes, which told me that she had been watching this whole encounter of mine unfold. In this moment, I also learned that she had the deepest of deep green eyes, the kind, if you recognize it, that you fall into and feel instantly connected, but very rare. Both of us were staring at each other; the "let's see who looks away first kind of moment" and… she does, just a glance, then those deep green eyes are right back on mine.

Excellent!

She probably already knew what I was going to ask because of my exchange with the old man and I knew if the book had been hers she probably would have already said but…

I asked anyway,

"Does this beautiful book by chance belong to you, Miss?"

Eye contact already made, she smiled politely yet with a hint of sexiness.

Clearing her throat slightly, she responded,
"Not as far as I can recall."
I found the answer uniquely~ peculiar...
Yet, it was satisfactory in determining I could sit.

Attempting an internal sigh, I set my bag down on the ground as I slid comfortably into the seat with minimal sound. Settling into my rest stop for the next two hours, I looked down on the book now lying in my lap.

My mind began to wonder about the green~ eyed girl, who was now to my right. My thinking began to conveniently drift and I began allowing the pages of the book to gently flow past my thumb. Creating a tiny soothing fan~like breeze as my thoughts roamed the spectrum of possibilities. The pages were soft and crisp to my fingers.

I realized I may have been doing my fluttering of pages for a few minutes at least, so I abruptly stopped and ran my fingers slowly down the front cover of the book.

It was an extraordinarily handsome book.

Deep tan leather with a unique looking small

gold-engraved ∞ in the bottom right-hand corner of

the front.

The binding looked like an antique journal yet it was still strong. As I breezed through the pages I saw that they were high quality, typed pages, like that of a professionally printed book.

Interesting!

I ran my fingers slowly down the front cover and read aloud the title written in gold font …*a story about god*

The leather cover felt peaceful and cool to the touch.

The thought crossed my mind about how aged the book's leather cover looked, yet the binding was solid and the pages were crisp. Whoever left this book took care of it … or seldom looked at it. I turned the book over and opened the inside looking for a copyright date but all I could find in the inside front of the book that looked anything like a date was

77… also in gold typeface, branded in about

sixteen point font on the bottom center of the inside cover.

Intriguing....

77... it looked very majestic with its thick goldenness.

I wonder what the 77 stands for? A date of print? A code of some kind maybe?

Either way an impressive book, obviously a mistake by someone but my gain, nonetheless. I might as well check out the inside of this book that I have been scanning and studying the surface of.

I have enough time at my disposal to read it... why not?

Let's see...

Four hundred and eight pages...

...seems like an easy read

The first page read-

CHAPTER TWO

Beginnings

Someone I once knew told me a story to pass to you… when the time was right.

Which is right now!

Here is your manual!

A chill ran down my spine as waves of consciousness passed over me.

Appealing I thought, *definitely catchy.*

As I turned to see what information page two would bring, I was strangely surprised to find a familiar card stuck between the thick, crisp pages of the book. Holding the card delicately between thumb and forefinger I read the familiar word...

Hybris

Surrounded by the black paint swipe making an imperfect circle and in the center of the card the green splatter...it was my card.

Flipping the card over... on the bottom of the back, I found my name-

Alex Walker
623-555-8925

Whoa!

That's bizarre- my card in this book.
One of my clients must have had this book.
I wonder who?

"Are you talking to me?" Green eyes sitting next to me, asked.

Startled, I chuckled and replied,
"I didn't realize I had been speaking out loud. Sorry, just a … talking to myself, I guess," I said, as I smiled and looked intensely at her lips, awaiting a response. Her mouth was slightly crooked and gave the appearance it smiled a lot.

Something was familiar about it, I liked it. That style of lips on a woman is my favorite. I focused on her even more intensely, letting my eyes travel from her lips, up her face until I was looking into those beautiful green eyes. I was struck with one word in my mind.

Stunning!

Her eyes, almond-shaped and large, had a perfect touch of innocence and playfulness. A heavy dose of knowledge seemed to be hidden beneath those dark, thick lashes and her eyes; they were green, so deeply green!

Not just green but brilliantly green...

Hers were the kind of eyes that allowed you to know that it is possible to stare into the soul of another being and get temporarily lost, pulled into their world and desire to know them at their core.

She took the card from my hand and read it, flipped it over, then back again.
She looked at me intently as she handed it back to me, "Do you know this guy?"

Her voice was spunky and melodically curious. A unique sensation overcame me as she passed the card back to me and our hands gently touched. In the form of a thought, a few moments of calm stillness occurred.

Then the notion that I had held onto for many years came to the front of my mind, a definition of love once given in a philosophy course I took-

Love -
A soul's recognition of its counterpart...
Then, whispering through my mind was my mentor from long ago...

Quiet and loud, peace and chaos are indeed balanced in the clear mind.

Pulling myself back, realizing I had yet to answer her, I responded,

"Umm… well… actually it's my card but I didn't put it here. I found it in this book; it seems to be just your everyday, ordinary coincidence."

"Really?" she asked, skeptical. "Your card in a book you found sitting in a seat in the middle of a crowded airport. That's a pretty big coincidence."

"Yeah, I guess so. It was probably a client of mine that had the book," I pondered aloud. Again I wondered who.

Glancing down at the book in my hands, I saw her hand, childishly, whisk it away.

Instantly allowing the thick pages to flip through her fingertips, just as I did, then grasping the book, opening to the first page and reading the words at a whisper,

"A story someone I once knew told me…to pass to you when the time was right. Which is right now!"

I saw the goose-bumps on her forearm; a sensation I had recently become reacquainted with as well.

Then, with a definite hint of attitude, she said, "Sounds pretty deep, probably better get to it."

And unconcernedly, she slid the book back into my hands, smiled, and returned to the magazine she was reading.

I panned my head slowly from left to right and was instantly reminded that I was in a crowded airport and a very full terminal. I felt attracted to this girl and...

I think she looks familiar... her lips...and those eyes- I wonder if I have met her somewhere before, maybe from ASU or maybe from one of the places I have lived since college.

But what just happened there? Something for sure, maybe she recognizes me?

Something was exchanged between me and Miss Green Eyes.

I could be mistaken but I am pretty sure, at the very least, she finds me intriguing...

Well, one can hope!

Sighing, I turned back to my own world.

According to the giant clock on the west wall, I had an hour and fifty-seven minutes until my flight boarded.

Judging by the thickness and the number of pages, I could finish this book and find out what flight green eyes was on. *Maybe I'll even strike up another conversation and learn more about her, in that amount of time, I might have to skip ahead some to accomplish all of that.*

I need to read, now with a purpose.

CHAPTER THREE

I skipped ahead to page eight to help my cause.

Eight began halfway down the page...

My entrance back into the world of the author began:

All things created will progressively travel through the time of eternity;

Before my eyes- as I exist in eternity as I shaped eternity. You should know and believe that truth and happiness are the agents of purification and that words are the lenses that focus the mind.

I am a Teacher.

    I always was and I always will be. I can teach anyone how to do anything they choose to learn. The most important concept for people to learn and realize fully is the existence and undeniability of the soul and the Truth of Existence.

    The truth to all questions can lie within these pages if a reader allows the Self to recognize those answers.

Well, that's an extremely deep beginning to a book, I thought—who wrote this?

I examined the book, turning it over in my hands.

There is not an author's name anywhere on here— strange!

    Bringing my head up, I thought about what a bold statement it was to make. I could think of a lot of questions that I would want the answer to; questions I had needed answers to for a long time but could this book really answer them for me?

    Can it really answer all questions? I seriously doubt it. I wonder if this book could tell me where

Miss Green Eyes lives or if she is just going to visit someone or maybe she is on a business trip.

Maybe she lives in the L.A. area somewhere.
She looks too relaxed in manner and dress to be going to L.A. for business.

But, curiously, I let the pages flip over my thumb, ahead again, to get a quicker glimpse into what this story was really about.

Page 18

Common Moral Consciousness

Could an organism with more than thirty billion years of biological engineering be false?

Our actions cannot be actions in reality   unless we choose them.

In acting morally we ought to take no account of consequences, only doing specifically what the <u>Right or True action is</u>; insisting merely that in deciding what we "ought" to do, our variable desires are irrelevant. All of these choices made by the masses and the results of these actions combine to create the common moral consciousness.

Ask yourself, where are we in all of this?

This is really deep I thought. I skipped ahead again, this time almost a quarter of the way through the book.

CHAPTER FOUR

Not <u>The</u> Beginning… but a beginning many years after.

On August 8, 1957, He was born into a family in Southern Arizona and one minute later, another was born in Northern Iowa. Each too far removed from their previously held knowledge of the Truth, each beginning their human existence unaware of the other.

The physical growing up will ultimately be the easy part; it will be the mental realizations that will be the most challenging-especially for Him.

Who is He?

This somewhat familiar feeling of curiosity urged me to flip ahead again; instead of going backward to find the answer, I decided to move ahead a good twenty pages.

The new page read-

So you want to know why?

If we are created after the first entity, caring and all powerful, shouldn't we be able to achieve all that He is?

God has realized that potentiality and soul development are no longer a given.

Development is a lengthy process, with many natural difficulties and distractions. The distractions are vast now, development is complicated and difficulties are everywhere.

This form of potentiality is in the god element and it needs to be developed and learned before it can be fully realized.

What if God were here, now, speaking to you and He asked what it was that would make you truly happy?

Would you know what the answer is to that question?

If He was here asking you, how do you find inner peace when the world around you is chaotic, would you have an answer?

Have you already found it?

Do you even know where to begin?

Think about why man has always searched for more than he has and strived to be more than he is.

Man is constantly Becoming.

Do you ever wonder why, in life, it is never enough; that something always seems to be missing?

What is it you are missing?

Knowledge of your true, fullest potential?

Have you even begun to figure out what it is?

The answer is right there.
All you have to do is reach in and.....

... GRAB onto IT!

Know It. In your soul.

Analyze your inner most secrets and learn who you are and who you want to be. Search to confirm for yourself the undeniable existence and limitless possibilities of the reality of truth in life. Becoming aware of this should comfortably push the limits of your mind far beyond anything you previously thought possible.

This process shouldn't be easy if you are doing it correctly. Do not get discouraged if things are rough and not easily understandable.

Remember patience, this can take some time and know that.

We are born into an imperfect world but perfection can be achieved.

Do you believe this is possible?

Perfection can be achieved in any isolated area, with any thing…if you understand that perfection is relative. It can be easy to achieve in the short term but the longer that we are here, the harder it becomes to maintain. It is important to understand that in any moment, you can be perfect.

Seek to align your Self with this perspective.

Know that at the very least perfection is possible in any moment, though it is not a necessary piece for understanding the whole.

Why is this important to know?

Being perfect gets more difficult over time, the more events that is presented to an individual to deal with, the greater the possibility to make a wrong choice or decision.

The primary objective is not to achieve perfection. Know that achieving perfection is a possibility; it is not the only goal but one of many.

Possible perfection or imperfection is a spectrum, it is meant to expose one of many possible paths available.

It especially and beautifully reveals the existence of the reality of truth in a physical form.

When considering all the options with this spectrum-why not choose to align ones decisions with doing what is right. Without knowing this truth, one may get lost and never even know to try. Understanding this is such a small part but one does need to start somewhere. Might as well start from the truth, it leads to far better futures.

True recognition and understanding of the existence and possibilities of the truth spectrum results in aligning one's life in the center area of the spectrum and this is self-fulfilling perfection. Where we choose to live in relation to that center determines what types of events we experience as we navigate through. This is the determining element in defining the life world...your personal reality.

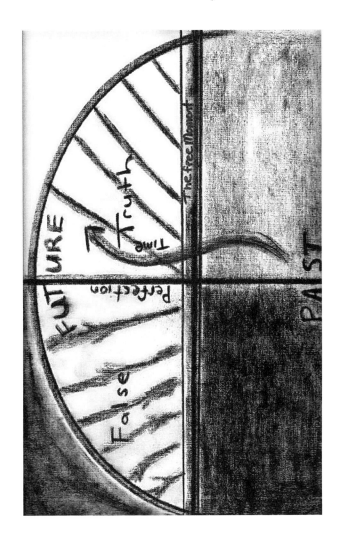

Each Individuals Spectrum of Truth

I was brought out of the books grasp by Miss Green Eye's melodic voice.

"It must be a good read, you seem really in to it," she commented.

I looked up into her eyes, then back down at the book.

"Yeah it's different. I am not really sure what it's about... really... yet anyway," I stumbled a little, still involved in the book but appreciating the opportunity to talk to her. And she initiated it! "I think the book is actually about God, like the title says."

I realized by her look this girl might snatch the book away again but curiously she didn't. Then, on the way up I noticed her lips and realized she must be using one of her best smiles because it is really cute and there is no way she is not aware of that fact.

She is absolutely flirting with me.

"It's definitely... interesting so far; I will let you know in about an hour." I glanced around the still full terminal and then turned back to her, "Where are you flying to?"

She fidgeted, shyly, with the rings on her fingers. I couldn't help but notice that she was

Introductions…a story about God

wearing several…but no wedding ring though, definitely a plus at this point.

Her response was good news…

"L.A."

Just as I suspected.

"Excellent…that's where I am off to as well. Where in L.A.?"

"Redondo Beach," she replied.

"Redondo Beach, huh? So, my next question is, of course, are you going home or going to visit?" I asked, crossing my legs and leaning in slightly for the answer.

"I am going home to my cat, Emmett," she responded with the cutest smile, fidgeting with her rings again.

Well, she is going home to her cat and she made a point of saying her cat and not a guy.

That's a good sign.

"You?" she asked.

Still very intrigued by her, I replied, "I am going on a little business vacation of sorts. I am going to L.A. for a week, then on to New York for a week to meet with some clients, I am a Process Development Consultant. With the vacation portion of my time in New York, I plan on trying to pitch a new book idea to a few publishing companies. I wrote this great

29

story and I hope to get it in print for a vast multitude of this world's population to read and enjoy."

I semi confidently grinned with a shrug, "Cool huh?"

"That is. Definitely!" she smiled at me, a thoughtful smile, "good luck with that!" She opened her magazine again and smiling, returned to her reading.

"Thank you" I said back to her, not able to help myself, I smiled back at her, then like that our moment ended and we returned to what we had previously been doing in the noisy terminal.

I shifted my eyes and interest back to the book. I had not marked my spot and apparently while speaking with Miss Green Eyes, I had closed the book.

So I quickly decided to guess on my location within this adventure and figured I had read approximately a quarter or so. I measured off about a quarter with my fingers and landed on page 153...

Okay, here we go.

CHAPTER FIVE

Adonae

I am Tristin and you have now changed my life and yours forever.

I grew up in several areas in Southern California but most of my life has been spent in all over the western part of the United States, going as far east as Iowa. My unhappy parents divorced when I was a young boy. The laws at the time placed me with my mother, even though the best place for me was clearly with my father.

My mother was unstable and relied on my grandmother to take care of her, my sister and me. She was also a woman who believed that it was the place she lived that was the problem and not herself and her choices. Because of this, my sister and I were uprooted many times, leaving behind any chance of real friends and stability.

Every summer and some holidays I would go visit my father, step-mother, and two brothers and every time I went back to my mom, she lived somewhere new. All the moving, back and forth, the instability, smothered any chance of developing a close relationship with either of my parents, or any of my siblings.

All my childhood and into adolescence I felt different and separate from all of my family, both sides, as if I didn't really belong. When I was not with my mom and sister, they had their own life and memories that I was not a part of. When I was not with my dad and brothers they functioned as a completely different family unit, with my brothers at the center of my dad and step-mom's world.

So which of these worlds was mine to call home?

Both?

Neither?

As a boy I can remember the yearning of just wanting to feel loved by my mom and dad. Hoping and praying that they just wanted to be around me, to spend time with me, to care about their son and what he thought and felt. I was so full of love with no one to share it with. I never felt that I was factored into their day or their life. However, none of this ever stopped me from wanting it.

At a young age I became aware of a god. It wasn't through a church or a religion but through a unique experience.

When I was seven years old, my grandmother paid for me to take swimming lessons at the local YMCA. It was such a great experience and I felt so lucky that I was able to be there. Having the opportunity to swim in a huge pool and have someone instruct me was something that was about me and no one else. I didn't have to share it with anyone.

One morning, after swim lessons, a flier caught my eye. It was about a weeklong camp in the mountains near Big Bear, California, for kids who went to the YMCA. When I saw the cost of $159, my excitement was deflated, knowing there was no way that I would be able to go.

My family did not have a lot of money and definitely would not pay for something as frivolously expensive as this. Extra, nonessential things were rarely allowed. As I read on, it said that you could sell cans of almonds through the YMCA to help pay for the camp.

A new hope flickered inside me.

Bound and determined and being on summer break, I got up early every single morning and went door to door, with my little red wagon, selling almonds throughout my neighborhood and all those around it. I went to so many different neighborhoods, set up shop in front of several grocery stores, and some nights I would have a little stand in front of my house for all the people driving home.

I continued every day for four weeks, right up until the money was due. I was determined to go to this camp and I was going to do it all on my own.

When I realized I had made enough money to go, I couldn't contain my excitement. That night in bed, I laughed almost to tears with happiness and excitement; feeling so grateful that I had done it. The excitement running through my body made it difficult to fall asleep that night but eventually I did. As I slept I dreamt about a beautiful place.

Two weeks later...An Event
Big Bear, California

When I arrived at camp, it was like nothing that I had ever seen. I had gone camping with my family before but this place was incredible. They had cabins with bunk beds for all of the campers to sleep in, with an Arts and Crafts cabin for daily activities and a dining hall where we ate. There was horse-back riding, lake swimming and canoeing, hiking trails, archery, and there was even a competition set up between all of the cabins; whichever cabin won the most games won the big trophy and dinner served by the other cabins. And of course there the bragging rights of knowing that you were the best! At nighttime, the entire camp would sit around a campfire, each cabin sitting together, and tell ghost stories, and roast marshmallows.

36

For me it was heaven, a safe haven, it was my new favorite place.

On the third day, we went on a day hike in the mountains to a place called Shoe-String Ridge. My friend, Mike and I, kind of got away from the group and started exploring the backside of the mountain. We both were off in our own world picking up neat walking sticks and unique rocks, pinecones and anything else we could find that looked cool. I had stopped by a tree to pick up a stick that would make the perfect sword, when Mike hurriedly called my name. I ran to catch up with him to see what he wanted to show me.

Almost to him, I slipped on pine needles and fell onto my backside. As soon as I hit the slick, pine-needle coated ground I started sliding, then began flipping head over heels down the side of the mountain.

Later I would learn it was a two hundred foot drop I had fallen down. I felt as though I was in a dream as I was flipping, and flailing, down the mountain, smashing into earth and rock. I zoned in or out for a moment and saw there was a man falling with me, as I slammed into rocks and dirt, then branches and bushes, and everything went black.

~*~

Everything was dark and silent and still.

Slowly a breeze came through and I could hear the sound of wind blowing through trees, rustling the leaves that lay on the forest floor.

I opened my eyes and all I could see was the swaying of trees above me, the sun shining through the clouds and down on to my body.

I tried to move but my body would not respond to what my mind was telling it to do.

I lay there, at the bottom of the mountain, on a bed of the very pine needles that had sent me hurtling down the massive hill, unaware of how much time had passed.

Am I dead? How would I know?

"No, Tristin, you are not dead," I heard suddenly, although the voice was affected by the ringing still going on in my ears. It did not come from somewhere, it came from within me. I opened my eyes to see a man standing over me.

How did he do that?

Blinking, I looked up at him and realized it was the same man who had tumbled with me down the mountain.

He kneeled, putting his hand on my shoulder, and said, "That was a pretty big fall. You should really be more careful where you step."

With a reassuring smile and a look of warmth and care, he walked away.

As I watched him fade into the forest, pain slowly started to seep into my body; I sat up and looked at myself, legs, hands and arms, covered in blood.

My face and my head hurt so badly.

"What happened to me?" I screamed, trembling from fear and exhaustion and pain.

I stood up, wobbly and bleeding, in shock. I tried to walk in his direction but could not.

Why was he leaving me?

Who was that guy?

I looked up at the sun, feeling its warmth on my face. I began to cry and tremble so hard and with a force that I had never experienced before. I hurt everywhere, inside and out and I was panicked. I started screaming over and over again, sweating now,

"HELP ME!"-scared that I wouldn't be found, lost, not knowing what to do.

I don't know how long I was there. It seemed like forever, before somebody heard me and began yelling back to try to locate exactly where I was. Finally two camp counselors arrived, exhausted and scared, I did exactly as I was told-lay down and relax. They examined me to see if I could be moved and determined that I could but the look on their face frightened me.

They carried me the entire, very long hike back to the camp medical office, which was normally a thirty minute brisk walk but between my extra weight and the apparent fragility of the situation, it took a lot longer.

By the time we arrived back at camp, it was dusk. I felt a little better and could tell it wasn't too bad. The examination by the doctor revealed only a few cuts, some scrapes, few large bumps and bruises.

Pretty lucky I was told, considering the fall I had taken. It was something that could have killed me but it didn't.

As a kid, you don't hold tight to memories like that, the vision of the man. Adults do not tend to believe you and after a while you move on, letting it flow to the back of your mind.

Children don't quite understand fully the concept of mortality so it made it difficult for me to grasp the concept of my own death. It wasn't until many years later that I realized how lucky I truly was to be alive after that fall and to have made it out without serious and permanent injuries.

~*~

The same thoughts and emotions came flooding back into my mind about eight years later, in the middle of winter. I was sixteen years old and I caught a glimpse of him again, the same man that had fallen with me down the mountain.

I was driving home from my girlfriend's house in Cherokee, Iowa in early January. The ground in this part of the country was blanketed with snow that had thawed and refroze a few times. Frozen snow and ice covered everything and on this night it was what I called bone-freezing cold outside. The roads were thick with black ice that looked like spun glass.

As I was driving, a gust of wind caught my car and as I pulled the car back to fight against it, I lost control. My mustang went into a spin that was still progressing down the road while gathering speed.

It was my first winter in this frozen part of the country and I had no idea what I was supposed to do. I started to spin toward the edge of the road, telephone poles coming at me. At that moment, I realized that I was completely helpless and there was nothing I could do.

There was a flash of light and a horrible sound-

SMASH!!!

Everything was still.

I looked up and saw the driver's side fender millimeters from slamming into a telephone pole.

It was in that instant, everything slowed and out of my passenger side window I made eye contact with the man before he turned and started walking away.

My mind started to spin, had I almost hit someone?

But it was below-zero outside; no one would be standing there on the side of the road in the middle of farmland.

As I went to get out of my car, I realized that it was saddled up to the snow piled waist high from the snow plows. I had to push the door with my feet to get it open.

By the time I was out of the car, the man was gone. I looked up and down the road but could see nothing. My heart and my mind were both racing as if they were going to explode.

Trying to collect myself, standing there in the middle of that icy, desolate road, frozen to the core, it suddenly occurred to me-with no seatbelt on, if my car had struck that pole at the speed I was going, I would have died right here on this frozen highway.

I began shaking from my core and started to cry, scared of what almost was. At this point in my life, I had become so protective of my feelings and emotions that I rarely, if ever, felt much of anything. The protective power I had over myself was the only real control I had in my life up until this point.

The feelings that began pouring out of my entire being that night changed the course of my life forever. Waves of helplessness of how I had felt as my car spun down the road, out of control continuously crashed over me until I felt as if I could no longer breathe.

I could have died right there, that would have been it for me.

Game Over!

Holy frickin' crap!

I was panicked.

I was in shock but gathered myself enough to realize that I needed to get to a phone and get some help. I began walking unsteadily down the road toward help that was at least five miles away. The shock of the accident plus the below freezing temperatures caused my body to shiver, uncontrollably.
Maybe someone will stop.
Who am I kidding? I probably won't even see another car out here at the this time of a cold night.
To take my mind off the distance and the cold, I started thinking about the man in the road.

Who was he?

Why was he standing outside of my car and why did he not stick around to help me?

Surely he would have thought I was in trouble and might need some help. He just stood there and watched then walked away.

Unless he wasn't really there to begin with?

No he was there, I saw him! I argued with myself.

There didn't appear to be much of an explanation why he would be there, on that frozen, empty stretch of highway. There was nothing out here but farmland with sometimes twenty miles between towns.

I made it to the end of the highway, where there was an old gas station with a payphone and decided it would be best to call my girlfriend instead of my mom. I knew my mom would be upset with waking her up and not happy with having to come and get me.

My girlfriend and her dad arrived about twenty minutes later and took me to my car.

"Whoa, Tristin!" her dad said, as he walked around the front of the car to the driver's side. "You are mighty lucky, son! You almost hit

that telephone pole, not to mention what this snow bank did to your vehicle. Are you sure you are alright?" he asked and turned to look at me.

My girlfriend came up to me as well and the two of them tried to nonchalantly examine me, looking for any external damage.

"No, I'm fine," I said, "just a little shook up and tired."

They looked me up and down again and once they were satisfied that I was not hurt or in any pain, we continued the process of hauling my car away from the telephone pole and out of the snow.

After what seemed like forever, we finally pulled up in front of my mom's house and unhooked the car. I thanked them for their help and after reassuring them once more that I was alright, I went inside and up to my room.

I put on a pair of old sweatpants and a long-sleeved-thermal shirt and climbed into bed. Pulling the covers up to my neck, I folded my hands behind my head. I just stared at the ceiling, thoughts swirling through my mind.

On one side, I couldn't help but think that I really, truly could have died. At the same time though, I recognized that I had walked away unscathed and shouldn't be too upset or concerned with how I had done this, only thankful that my life had not ended.

So many questions and thoughts were surging through my mind about life, death and about God.

Why am I here?

Who is God?

What happens when we die?

Where do we go?

How is all of this, the world, the universe, possible?

How are we supposed to live?

Why are any of us here? Is there a purpose?

And then it hit me.

I had all of these questions but I didn't have any answers. I needed answers. But where do you try to find answers to the kinds of questions that I was now lying alone, nervously anxious, in bed with?

How do I find out-

Who am I?

Why or how did I get so lucky tonight to still be here?

I was a sixteen year old kid that meant nothing to no one. Why is it that I am the product of a dysfunctional, divorced family? How could two people make a child together and then not care enough about that child to show him they loved him or try a little harder to stay together to teach him what a family is, the way I think a child should be raised?

God must have something more in store for me than this life I am currently living, to have given me the opportunity to continue to be here.

I was still awake at dawn, so I went out on the front porch and watched the first rays of sunlight touch the Earth, still so much on my mind. It occurred to me that this was the first time that I had ever sat and watched the sun come up.

It was perfectly beautiful and peaceful.

I could not imagine a sunrise more perfect than the one that I saw the morning after the night I almost died.

The early morning sky was magnificent and calming. Light pink and orange swirled together like sherbet, with splashes of yellow thrown in.

As the first rays of sun were dancing onto the Earth in front of me, my mind began to clear and I realized that I needed to understand some things better, to get some answers to some big questions. That there were questions to be answered and it was not accurate to live your life ignorant about these things, it cannot be what God wanted.
One thing finally was for certain to me.

I mattered.

I may have to prove to them all that I do but I felt it at the core of my being that I was going to do something great with my life and who I am. I had no idea what it would take for me to reach my ultimate goal but I would.

That was the day that I started consciously on the path that would eventually lead me to understand who I am, what I must learn, what I must do and how to be.

At some point in your time here, this moment must be achieved to truly gain an understanding for the gift of life and your purpose here.

CHAPTER SIX

As my life continued, I moved myself in the direction of finding these answers. I knew the best place for me to start would be by going to college. It wasn't a degree that I desired, it was the knowledge that I craved. I wanted the answers.

It was about halfway through my freshman year, when I met someone who helped me travel that road of knowledge that led me to some of the answers. He was a Teacher and although his time in my life was short, the wisdom he left me with was immeasurable.

I was walking across the grass, enjoying the coolness of the morning, allowing myself to let my mind drift not really thinking about anything.

Something about him caught my eye. He was walking toward me, as if he knew me, knew who I was but I couldn't easily tell if he was someone that I recognized.

As the distance between us narrowed, his face became clearer and my heart raced, my mind wondering if he was friend or foe.

Wait! Don't I know him?

Our paces quickened as we walked toward each other, I wasn't going to veer off and neither was he. Then, my mind and the moment slowed and I realized that I felt safe with this man, that I felt like I knew him. I didn't know how but I knew that he was good.

I was drawn to him in a way that I had never felt about another person before. I could feel his energy. He was about 6'2" with a medium build and light-brown hair. He appeared to be in his mid-forties but still had his youth. His face was peaceful and kind with warm, brown eyes, holding wisdom in them unlike anything I had ever seen. The slight lines around his eyes and mouth suggested that he smiled a lot.

The whole moment told me that he meant no harm. When we were a few feet from each other, he smiled and said,
"Hello Tristin."
My mind flashed back to a moment in time that I would never forget. I saw the image of the man standing next to my mustang on that frozen, deserted road. This man was there the night that I almost died two years ago………
I shook my head, no it couldn't be.
"I know you?" I half asked, half said.
"Do you?" He asked back with a smile.
"I feel like I do anyway but I am not sure. Who are you?"

A clumsy yet seriously cheerful and energetic looking little girl about six years old brought me back out of the book, as she stumbled over my feet. We apologized at the same time and exchanged a similar unconcerned smile and shrug. Although her shrug was accompanied by one eye brow raised at me; cute but possibly intended to be ornery... probably a real handful at home.

Nonetheless...

Looking at the giant, clock on the wall-

I saw that I have been rather deeply engrossed in this book for almost twenty more minutes. I did tell green eyes that in an hour I would let her know whether the book was any good or not.

I should get her name when I give her my book analysis

...almost out of nowhere I was compelled to speak.
"The book is good so far, by the way," I said, turning to her and giving her a little head nod.
Her reply was short but still with a great smile, "Sweet!"

"Sweet!" I said back, fumbling over my thoughts, "I mean that's sweet that you say sweet because I do too. It's pretty cool, I mean. My name is Alex, what's yours?" I extended my hand to meet hers and we slid our hands into a comfortable grasp.

Love is a souls recognition of its counterpart in another my mind whispered.

She squeezed my hand and replied,
"Lisa"
Wow, she is beautiful!
I think I have seen her before. She is familiar looking.

54

Those eyes are tempting to look at.

Realizing we were still shaking hands, I slowly pulled mine from hers, smiling the entire time. Still nodding to each other, our eyes slowly drifted back to what we were doing and with a momentary giggle, we shrugged and continued on with our airport distractions.

Again, I seriously think she likes me.

Scanning the crowd around me, I smiled to myself then turned my full attention back to the book.

Dang it! I didn't mark the page again.

This is going to be the most interesting way I have read a book ever. So I guesstimated again... well, page 198 looks good, again simply one word was found.

Matthew D. Harding

CHAPTER SEVEN

Jon

As I stared at the name for a few minutes, I kept thinking about the fact that there was something about this girl's beauty; it was calm but bright, deep and real. I still think I might know her from somewhere.

I just can't place it.

I have got to finish this book!

Shaking my head in an attempt to clear it, I turned the Jon page.

The next began with-

I am Jon

To most that statement holds no significance. But the truth is that it should hold some, as I am the second god to ever come out of the mist, a dear and close friend of the Creator of Eternity. I was the first to bear witness to all that He has created, I am the first god that was taught all the knowledge that He had gained since coming out of the mist.

I can still remember the feeling that grew inside of my being as He spoke to me, his words becoming pictures that I could see, pictures that I could feel.

He taught me how to develop my eternal soul. With such excitement, he showed me and I eagerly learned, all that he had realized. Such things as: Growth and development exist chaotically, peacefully and perfectly throughout all of eternity; the truth spectrum, and the eternal reality.

Once, while walking together, He shared with me an idea.

"I waited more than eight thousand years before you realized who you were, Jon." He said to me. "Who knows how long we were in there before I realized myself. How many of us could *be inside the mist? I think the numbers could be endless!"*

"But the possibility exists that maybe we are it," I replied, slowly.

Even as I said it to him I could feel the falseness of my own words deep inside and I knew that was not the correct answer.

He said it aloud, in his calm, prepared, yet excited way,

"I don't think so-Look at the size of it. Even with all that I have created, it only takes up a fraction of the space that the mist does."

I looked at the mist.

It was indescribable!

Translucent like water and vapor that held small grain-like particles; inside floated what looked like bubbles filled with something.

That something pulled at me and I could tell it pulled at Adonae. I turned to look back at Adonae. It spread throughout eternity with no beginning and no end and limitless space. The tiny, bubble-type entities floated peacefully and perfectly throughout the mist, occasionally bumping into one another yet each on their own path.

"Well, coming out of the mist is obviously a tremendously complicated accomplishment," I

reasoned with him, vague memories, feelings, it had indeed been a difficult process.

"Jon, I have thought of a way to get more out of this mist."

"How?" I asked, tentatively.

"By going into the mist and trying to communicate with the others, possibly we would be able to encourage or compel them to follow us out. I think that whatever is inside those bubbles is where we begin, that we need to help them realize that they are more than just that bubble, that they can be what we are. "

"Adonae, have you considered the possibility that coming out of the mist is a disruption of some sort? That maybe it throws off the balance somewhere inside; that maybe it creates waves of turmoil, or disorder throughout this entire place? Which would mean that going in and then back out could be difficult and possibly chaotic."

He paused for a moment before answering and looked at me with such thoughtful, sincere eyes then said,

"I have given this such deep, long, focused thought and I keep finding the same answer: that I overwhelmingly feel a positive desire to create beauty and life in as much as I can. I want to love and help others know what I know. If it were

wrong to come out of the mist, we, two good beings would not have found a way out."

"I believe that if there are more of us in the mist and they could realize what we have, they would want to be where we are."

I thought for a moment and realized that I agreed with Adonae on helping others to be here, that what he said was true.

"But how do we do it?" I asked, rather loudly, still hearing the hesitation in my voice.

"Simple," He said, "We walk in as far as we can go and try to communicate in every way we know and I believe they will listen and follow us. I believe that we have the understanding and the knowledge within us. They will hear this, they will feel it and know that we speak the truth."

"How do you know that once we go back in, that we will be able to get back out ourselves?"

"Ummm…well, we should not go in too far at first, proceed cautiously, until things become clearer. Jon, I don't know any of this for sure; I am figuring this entire thing out as I go. I feel certain this is the right thing to do. Something tells me we will be able to come back out if we choose."

I took a deep breath and nervously said, "Okay, let's try it......"

Going in to the mist was effortless; trying to get the bubble-type substances to listen was not.

How we originally helped them out of the mist was done more with an overwhelming feeling and thoughts rather than words. Those that came first dripped off of us. We showed the 'bubbles', the world that existed outside the mist. They became Gods. We showed them ourselves and all that we had realized and all that we had become. We showed those first few in our raw, unprepared and honest way, the truth. We helped them feel all the emotions they could feel.

Through all of these things they were able to understand they existed outside of the mist. Although most chose to stay, content with their existence.

The existent power involved in being born into eternity and realizing yourself as a god was almost limitless but it would later prove to have some unexpected boundaries.

Whereas for so long it appeared we had none, it was then found that realizing yourself out of the mist allowed you to exist solely in the god realm.

Later, we learned that by being born, physically, inside a planet's atmosphere, you could potentially obtain the skill of being able to move between worlds. Actively interacting with a physical world is an amazingly spectacular event.

Initially, all we were trying to do was get others to come out of the mist and live in beautiful eternity with us. Once we learned how to exist physically, the game changed for many of us. There was something new to perfect.

Things went well for hundreds of thousands of years, with hundreds and hundreds of gods coming out of the mist, some with our help and some on their own by realizing their truth just as Adonae and I had, existing, recognizing, experiencing, loving and learning in eternal beauty and harmony of the eternal world…

Those few gods that realized their own existence outside the mist, without our help, have always shared this unique bond with one another and a deeper understanding of truth and the joy of being.

Many gods were choosing to exist physically, more often. For his own reasons, Adonae never did. I believe He felt it would limit Him or trap Him. He so loved the freedom of eternity.

CHAPTER EIGHT

Love

It was as close to perfection as one could get.

However, with so many gods, it was certain that another bold god would come up with a different idea for creating life to experience reality, to live and enjoy. We only knew life that had been born from the mist. Even those born into a physical world first came from the mist and they grew up safely, knowing they were a god because they were taught everything, which even in the beginning was a considerable amount of information. They were all properly prepared for their eternal experience.

The idea of creating new souls came from the god named Sebastian. Sebastian, early on, was a wonderful, young creative god that tried hard to get the attention of Adonae. He was always devising new ideas and new creations to share with Adonae that he felt would make things even better. I think they were destined to collide.

But at this point in time, Adonae spent his time with his beloved Elizabeth, exploring creations and the place he created named Drifter's Paradise. The paradise was truly the most complex and beautiful creation ever realized. Now it had become his lone desire and passion to be with Elizabeth most of the time. His time as a teacher of gods had, for the most part, passed. He still wrote but spent the majority of his time exploring and experiencing the universe with Elizabeth. Other gods knew this and understood.

For some reason, Sebastian felt slighted by not being raised by Adonae, as I and many of the other first gods had been. He did not realize that Adonae was a part of him, just as he was a part of all of us. He loves us all and we are all connected to him in a uniquely infinite way. It was He who compelled us to Be, to realize who we were and therefore, realize ourselves out of the mist.

Not all, but most newly realized gods are raised by a group of young gods, who were raised by Adonae, Elizabeth, and I.

Adonae had stopped actively participating in the soul development aspect a long time ago. We still run the same processes He developed and used, all the same lessons, all the same preparation and love.

I mainly oversee and confirm that all things are going the right way. Occasionally there are dilemmas, but very few in the eternal realm. Those few have always been huge.

Eventually, Sebastian took this 'new soul' idea to Adonae in a private setting. The next day Adonae spoke to everyone and explained what He thought.

The decision was made unanimously not to support Sebastian's idea to create new souls and this led to Sebastian's decision to garner support in favor of his idea amongst the masses of other gods. No one had ever opposed Adonae before.

Sebastian did not obtain the support of one other god to stand with him in the presentation of his idea. All knew that if creating new souls-new mystic life forms- were the right thing to do, then Adonae would have been in favor of it.

Every single god knew that Adonae only wanted everyone to experience love, the Truth about the eternal living reality.

This embarrassment, as Sebastian took it, caused him to feel things no other god had ever felt. There was badness in him, there was a sadness he should not have felt, a falseness never before realized. He should not have expected Adonae to accept something that was false. But he did.

Nonetheless, because of Sebastian's falseness, Life would be created by combining elements of our eternal selves and the physical uniqueness that we had created.

For a long time, this life, sadly, was created and stranded, mentally void of godly knowledge or experience. They were never told that they were gods and by being closed off from the rest of us, they did not even know that this potentiality existed. And we did not know that they existed for a long, long time.

It was wrong for them to exist under this pretense and sad to learn that it was possible.

Sebastian hastily decided to come visit me and while there he shared with me all that he had researched and done to develop this idea and why he could see it as truth. No matter the words I used or the truth of what it was, he could only see the benefit of his idea. According to him, if there could be new souls created outside the mist, that meant there was life elsewhere besides the mist. This life equally deserved to realize its Self-like nature like all other gods were given the opportunity to do.

Sebastian was ignorant to how Adonae or any of the others could not see the beauty in creating new life. Sebastian failed to see the eternal truth that Adonae is such that he can only, by choice, affirm the truth because of his knowledge and experiences. You could trust and count on Adonae's leadership. If it is not a truth, Adonae will not be able to support it.

Therefore I cannot support it, I explained to him. I asked him to let it go and explore and create with us.

So, angry, humiliated and with his young, god mind, he secretly created the first new souls to be born into existence. The new life was born in a beautiful corner of the Drifter's Paradise, in two pairs.

Sebastian attempted to raise them as Adonae and I had raised the other gods. He gave them knowledge and taught them through words and allowed them to experience what he wanted them to know. At first, unbelievably so, the new life beings grew exactly the same way the gods grew. The reality and truth of it is that they were gods, they were the same as us, they just didn't know it yet... They didn't know to realize it and no one taught them the truth about reality.

They grew up and bore new life, and their offspring bore more, continuing this cycle for many, many years. Sebastian taught them many things including all about Adonae and the history of all the first gods.

As his first level grew, they asked often of getting to be in the presence of gods. This put Sebastian in a difficult position. He knew Adonae and the other gods would not be happy about these new life creations because he had gone against what Adonae had believed to be the truth. So to buy himself more time to figure out how to tell Adonae, Sebastian made the cataclysmic mistake and told these new beings, these new souls, that they were not yet ready nor were they worthy enough to meet the other gods; that they must first realize certain truths in order to be worthy. He manufactured the idea that he was the one true god and he would decide who was worthy and no other god would be worshipped but him.

Instead of teaching all the truths he knew, he held back valuable information and made it so that they had to figure it out on their own in order to be with the gods. This knowledge was taught to all other gods immediately after coming into existence. Never did Sebastian tell them this crucial piece of information. Nor that they too were gods they had the potential to live as a god. If they could learn as a god, they too could be for eternity; their life and existence was limitless.

This lack of knowledge was the only difference between those Adonae compelled out of the mist and those Sebastian brought to the beloved Drifter's Paradise.

In a small corner of paradise, he raised a new type of god…the lost god.

The intellectual detail of the method designed by Adonae was beautiful. This beauty was not understood and utilized by Sebastian in creating this new life. The physical bodies that Adonae developed were perfect. They allowed for growth and development; the mind contained the actual life being and it too allowed for optimal and necessary growth, development, and advancement.

All the gods that have come out of the mist have the ability to exist eternally, once physically experienced, on the human level. The fully realized ones true Self can exist on either realm, at any time.

Sebastian's idea for existence, unfortunately, has another problem. It can be manipulated for control purposes because the education and development of the soul is not interwoven into their being from the beginning. Trying to add it later just results in a layering effect, making it much more difficult to result in the pure, true connectedness of Adonae's method and godhood.

All things are in a balance- truth and falseness do exist.

The eternal god being has one level of consciousness and it goes in all directions, for all eternity. However, if you are born into existence in a physical world, whether it is to realize your Self out of the mist or just for the spectacular experiences of it, you start life as an infant Self that has to develop, learn, and grow. Adonae realized that it would be dangerous to have this empty memory bank filling up on the same conscious level as it is on in eternity. Too much information coming in too fast, leads to confusion within the human mind.

Therefore, Adonae created another level of consciousness for the physical human experiences to be recorded alongside the god level of consciousness. Two parallel levels, each having the same forms of experience: sight, smell, touch, sound, taste, thought, eternity.

The only problem with this process is that Sebastian realized a way to suppress the realizations so his creations never realized who they truly are and thus has imposed a thought pattern on them that can and has developed into enslavement and self-sacrifice.

Sebastian began realizing this strategy back when he had first developed new life. He had to postpone their requests to meet the other gods by telling them that they had to learn more before they would be ready for that eternal gift. Immediately, he began studying the results and discovering new methods to advance this idea.

Having studied this strategy of control, Sebastian decided to try this new method on his original life forms, then on his current creations that were still being born into existence at a very high rate. It worked.

Unfortunately, he has been successful in implementing this strategy into life for a very long time. Sebastian's control is his consciousness released as waves of sound, light, and even thoughts and it comes at everyone here, from all directions.

It is the distractions that take you away from the Truth. They are very clever and mostly hidden from understanding.

Sebastian has now, today, been successful in covering the entire place with his web of confusion and because of its enormous impact, very few gods have returned from the place formally known as Drifter's Paradise; now a lost paradise.

Only the re-experiencing gods actually have the natural ability to make it out and even at times, they have not been able to make it back. Those lost during re-experiencing are still trapped within this reality and they develop a thought process that becomes layered and built into the experience...it becomes their false reality for eternity.

Everyone born on Earth is a god but they have no memory of this fact. This makes their chances highly unlikely of realizing they are and "getting out". If they do not realize, or have a memory of being a god, then the 'godly' powers are not awakened and it lies dormant in their soul until such time that they do realize. The difficulty in doing this and the fact that there are virtually no teachers available here to receive and help develop a god, makes the process hidden and incomprehensible.

Sebastian created the ability for there to be a lost soul, therefore, it is a possible Truth now.

In the beginning, once it was discovered that Sebastian had created new life; other gods of Adonae's were born here as babies in attempt to become proper teachers for those lost due to Sebastian's ignorance.

Many were not originally taught by anyone as they grew up, they realized that they were a god, that they were not limited by the physicality of the Earth, of this world in which they now lived.

They diligently worked to teach those lost Gods who had continually been being born into one body after another since the beginning of this. They were gods and they too could experience eternity and love. Once a realized soul had passed in this world, they returned to eternity with the other gods. A majority of them would continue to go back and try to help the other lost gods that didn't even know to try for anything beyond the physical limitations of this Earth. Trying to realize themselves back into eternal existence and reality was confusing. The Truth is something else existed though, something wonderful, something they didn't truly know about or couldn't fully understand. They didn't understand what it meant or what they were missing. They could sense it in other Gods but were confused as how to get it themselves.

In existence there must be a balance between truth and falseness, this is an eternal fact that began development when Adonae first realized Himself out of the mist. Although he didn't notice it for many, many years.

These gods who always knew they were gods did not realize, could not possibly comprehend, the evilness that was developing to keep the balance. Gods born and raised without ever knowing they were gods, possibly could learn to have, feel and perpetuate this evilness to others.

This time I was brought out of the book and into this current reality by the old guy next to me and his elbow going into my side; I think he did it on purpose. I stared at him but he wouldn't look at me. I wondered if I was reading out loud again but still not a reason to hit someone like that.

Nonetheless, rude if it was intentional, but I am not going to get into it by saying something. It might have been an accident but pretty hard for unintentional and no apology. I may need to pay a little more attention to this grey-haired, crossword puzzle character next to me.

WOW! I thought. *This book is really deep. This is God stuff, like the beginning of all time stuff!*

I glanced at the giant clock on the wall and saw that I was forty-three minutes into this book. I briefly deliberated about the fact that I was enjoying the reading and a feeling of amazement and nervousness; an almost anxious feeling came over me. It's an interestingly, entertaining read.

This is unlike anything I have ever read before. It is a unique storyline leaving me feeling intellectually entertained and curious as to what else was going to come out of this book. But it is frustrating me, for some reason, and I just want to chuck it across the terminal.

It is so matter-of-fact and direct, as if it is telling a story, that is very important, but just the base, just the *Introduction*. This book leads me to believe that I am actually reading about God.

How could it be though? I mean a book about God, left sitting on an empty seat in terminal B-8?

Right!

It's good!
But I need to finish it also.
Back to the book and ahead a few pages.

CHAPTER NINE

I was Tristin.

My search for Ultimate Reality was long and at times beyond difficult but it led me to the Truth. A truth that had I not learned from my teacher, as young as I did, I may never have survived the struggles I have been a part of.

In the end, I learned that it could have been so much easier to embrace but the reality of this world is designed and intricately developed to hinder any such discovery. The reason for this is that the reality of this world is developed out of fear, uncertainty, and greed. It needs mankind's combined consciousness to exist; we are the combined creators of the experienced human consciousness.

Everything exists because it was thought about or done by someone here. This was not created somewhere else and brought here; this was created here on Earth.

It must be understood that the discovery of an Ultimate Reality or Truth is possible.

One must start with this premise:

If you can listen with the openness necessary and find your own path to discovering the Truth, you will become wholly aware of another possible world; a world free of anger and hate, pain and suffering, a world where any form of falseness could never exist. Just because evil or untruths are real and logical possibilities does not mean that you have to choose them.

The most powerful characteristic is the ability to freely choose an untruth or a morally evil act in any form and instead refrain and choose the truth, the right action, every time. An alignment of one's Self with the divine way must be freely chosen or the truth will never be realized and the individual will become lost.

I was certainly not the fastest or the most graceful of humans but I was on a mission to find answers because someone I trusted showed me how and why I needed to learn who I was.

I am a product of this Earth.

I, of course, struggled intolerably at times yet other times I found the journey effortless, exciting, and full of love. I felt comfortable and at home with my life.

Some of my many teachers along the way tried to reveal to me the variety of options available to perceive the world but there was only one way that could reveal its Truth from the inside out and at the same time remain complete.

This truth exists in every moment, in every being. Each event in life is a building block to discovering the truth, while at the same time discovering the true Self and the incredible reality of mine and your place in the history of time.

I remember the moment I truly began the process of realizing who I AM

It was Tucson

It was a beautiful, clear, sunny morning down by the pool. The pool was sparkling and the hot tub was bubbling. It was a large, beautiful hot tub built with Spanish tile all along the border. The sounds of birds chattering filled the air. The distractions of the everyday world had yet to find me or this place and I felt at peace.

A baby wren awkwardly attempted a landing on the handrail intended to guide ones way into the hot tub. Immediately after landing her little feet on the gleaming chrome, she began her descent into the hot, steamy water.

I watched initially with the thought that maybe she knew what she was doing- the way she skid sideways into the tub, with feathers out she looked like she had done this before. Once she hit the water, immediately came the flailing and the flapping of wings as she attempted to fly out of the clutches of the steaming bubbles. I knew this wren did not intend to be in this hot water with me.

A moment of choice was presented; a moment that possibly reveals a person's true character.

I slowly glided over to the tiny flailing wings and stuck my hand out to the wren. Without any hesitation, she jumped onto my first knuckle. I gently lifted her out of the water a bit, expecting her to fly away- but she did not. Moving slowly over to the decking, I laid my hand on the damp ground to let her climb off but she chose to stay on my knuckle.

With her head crooked, she stared into my eyes and I could feel that she was not afraid of me. It is in the nature of all living things to fear the unknown...yet to her I was not unknown. After a few precious moments, she chirped softly, her way of a thank you, I assumed. She fluttered her wings, and flew away with one last chirp.

I sat there, watching her fly, sensing that something inside me had transformed; something had changed for the better, unaware of exactly what yet.

Enlightenment-

What does it feel like?

I was eager to inform Jon of my realizations. I think he had been waiting for this, such a simple, pure moment that revealed so much to me.

The paradise revealed and the enlightenment process understood.

It was late on a Saturday afternoon, a warm breeze ruffling the cherry blossoms of the trees in Jon's private paradise.

Everywhere was lush green grass blended with the vibrant colors of the flowers and bushes. There were tall hedges around this breathtaking place that made up the maze that that led to the center, Jon's garden.

At the center of the garden, was a fountain, not extravagant but simple. I think it was mostly there for the sound of the water more than the appearance. We were sitting at a little table in one of the corners, drinking a glass of freshly squeezed and very pulpy lemonade, enjoying the peacefulness we were able to obtain by being in this sacred place.

On the journey out here I had noticed Jon carrying the book but had forgotten it until that moment. I looked over to Jon but my attention was caught on the book itself, lying on the table between the two lemonade glasses. I picked up the book and turned it over in my hands, feeling the leather of the cover, the durability of the binding. Turning it back over, the title leapt out at me, as always, 'Steps to Enlightenment'.

I love this book!

I flipped through the book and stopped at a page in the middle. It looked like an easy place to start, a page filled with numbers.

I skipped to 22- it had caught my eye.

Step 22-

Understand who you are and what this world is actually like. All around there are falsifiers to create the illusion of what is going on. This is not always the reality or the truth. Pull it apart, look at it closely and examine it for what it truly is. Then turn inward and do the same to yourself, to your soul. Identify the illusions that exist in your life world. Develop strategies to remove the illusions that exist and you will come out with the complete understanding of who you are at your core.

Be honest!

<u>Step 23-</u>

Ask yourself what your place is in this world-there is a place for everyone-a place that they feel the most comfortable and connected… happy.

What is your part?

What do you offer to this world?

Are you a creator or a destroyer?

Again, be honest, even if it hurts!

<u>Step 24-</u>

What do you want your place to be in this world?

Who do you want to be?

This is a question of your eternal character-are you a being that is good and ethical?

Who are you at your core?

In your life on this paradise, you may make bad choices and decisions but it is your responsibility to learn from them and choose the right choice the next moment. The most important thing is to be happy with your place in this world. Because you know that you chose it. You might be born in to a very difficult position or a very blessed situation but what you do with it is entirely up to you. Your place is what you make it. You get to decide.

Know what is important to you, then go out and get it and keep it.

Be honest.

Instantly my mind raced as it began to think about the processes and cycles in my own life.
What were they?
Did I have a place?
What was it if I did?
What did I want to be?
Then it was there~

Clarity

Something suddenly made sense, a missing piece in my puzzle just fit.

I could feel things clicking, falling into place.

Everything was making so much more sense.

This book was speaking a truth. It touched something in the back of my mind, my heart, and my being.
I was becoming…shall I dare say enlightened!
I think I know what it feels like now.
I asked Jon,
"Where did you get this book? I don't see a publishing company or writer's name on it anywhere."

"A friend put it together for me a long time ago," Jon replied.

Satisfied enough with the answer, I turned inward to the hundreds of questions racing through my mind, then asked,

"Is there more going on here? Is there more that we are not aware of? I have always felt like things are not complete here, that we don't even come close to the knowledge we could have."

"Of course there is. There is far more going on than I believe the ordinary human mind can comprehend, Tristin."

"What? What is going on? What are you saying? You are being so vague. Sometimes I feel like maybe you think I should already know what you are talking about, that I should already know something that I don't."

"Most people go through all their individual lives completely lost and too scared to live and especially scared to die. Someone needs to teach them, while they are here, how to feel again and how to love again. It is possible to be happy every single day again," Jon said, with a hint of sadness in his voice. *"It has been a long time."*

I studied Jon for a moment, organizing my thoughts and feelings, trying to figure out what I was even trying to ask. The moments ticked by and then I finally spoke,

"There is something you have been leading up to while teaching me and helping me to grow. What is it?"

"You have a great deal yet to realize, Tristin."

"So many times in my life you have been there to protect me, why?"
With a slow, amused chuckle, Jon said,

"Oh, Tristin, I was merely watching, observing, taking notes. You were protecting yourself. You are in control of your world"

"How? How was I protecting myself? I couldn't possibly protect myself from those incidents. You were there, I saw you. Every time it was a situation in which I should have or could have been killed. I walked away, completely fine. That couldn't be by my doing that would take something bigger than me to do that. Look like I said, you were there, out of nowhere. What are you? Just tell me are you a guardian angel or something?"

He studied me for a moment and then shook his head,

"No I am not. Although what truly is a guardian angel or any kind of angel? Aren't they merely gods caught watching over humans? Maybe they once were human and therefore understand what humans are going through?"

"Ok, that could make sense but what stops you from being that? Are you a human angel, I mean what are you?" I asked, "Because I know you are not human, not exactly anyway, maybe you were once."

"Tristin, this is going to be complicated how ever it goes, I guess. Soon you will understand it all-I know this. Just give yourself the necessary time for growth and understanding. This is the only way that it will work, I have figured that much out by now. Besides, who or what I am is not a necessary piece of information for all that you are trying to understand and to learn. I am merely a Teacher, here to help guide you through this time and give you the tools, as needed, to help you process new information. Ultimately, all that I teach is already known, it is just for you to decide what to do with that knowledge. The question is not who I am but who you are. Who are you, Tristin? Are you different from me?"

I thought about it for a minute, then responded,

"Well, I don't really know who I am or if I am different from you. This is what I am trying to figure out. Sometimes I feel so close but the answers seem to be just outside my reach and I just don't get there. It can be very frustrating! And then I wonder am I trying to figure out what

kind of person I want to be morally and ethically or am I trying to figure out who I am because I have forgotten."

I sighed, sitting back, feeling baffled by the entire moment.

Jon looked at me as if he was trying to see something. I was not sure what he was looking for but a small smile told me that he was amused.

Then he said to me,

"Answer me this-What is it you think about the most? What is it that you want the most?"

I pondered this question for a moment.

"Well," I began, "I would say that I think about happiness and being happy the most. I want to be happy in this world, no matter what. I think about enjoying life, really enjoying it and having others enjoy their lives. I want people to learn how to be happy and how to stay happy. It is possible, Jon, and you know it is."

"You see, Tristin, the problem is that most people out there don't even know what real happiness is. They spend their whole lives miserable inside because although they are drawn toward the light of the truth, society and culture shoves them in the other directions-so they stay semi-unaware of their potential intended course."

"This is what I want to change about the world. I believe people can be happy every day, even though they have to freely choose it at every moment." I said.

I got up from my chair and walked around, lightly touching the flowers, inhaling the clean air and many different aromas, admiring the breeze and its ability to gently caress everything it blew by.

"How can you not be happy, when there are possible moments like this? It really is about taking the time to stop and·smell the roses, or flowers in this instance. When you can appreciate the little things and respect the big things, you recognize that there really is no difference between them because they are both just things, amazing and equal."

I lay down in the grass, propped up on my elbow and stared at Jon, eager to hear his response.

Jon looked thoughtful for a moment, then looked down at me, indecision in his eyes.

"I don't know if any one individual can change the world at this point, certainly not alone anyway. People have to want to change or at least be open to the possible good that they hear and see. They need to let those things impact their lives, especially their actions.

Such a high percentage of the world's population is controlled by the news, religion, and government; Controlled by fear and greed, with a lot of selfishness. I believe they have grown to love their misery because so many don't believe in anything else. They don't believe that happiness, love, and peace are actually, constantly possible."

"Fine, I understand it might be thought of as impossible and the odds are certainly stacked against it. But why is it that I have such an overwhelming desire to change the world, inside me? This desire is accompanied by an equally strong belief that it can be done and that I could do it."

"Maybe someday you will be able to answer that question… better than me, I hope." Jon said this in a way that revealed a sign of sadness to me. This was a strange side of him that I hadn't seen before.
Why?

He then got up and walked over to the fountain, staring down at the water and the reflection it held, which signified that he needed to think.

I began to look through the book again, pleased but slightly troubled about the conversation we had just had, letting my mind drift to my own thoughts about what he had said *and what he had asked me. As I flipped through, I noticed a page that had a hand-written passage. I have always loved to read handwritten stuff in books; it is like a glimpse into the author's private world. It makes the story itself become more real. Knowing this book was already a one-of-a-kind written by Jon's friend, made it even more intriguing.*

Who is Jon in all of this?

Dreaming and Screaming

We spend countless hours of our short lives searching for something, anything, to help us feel happy and satisfied. Many people enter the old age period of human life, full of regrets, sadness, and pain. For they have never found what it was that would make them feel whole.

Why is this?

The answer to the riddle is inside you; it cannot be found out there in the chaos of the world.

You are the key that unlocks all doors.

So unlock them all.

I closed the book.

Despite the warm breeze, I felt a shiver of Truth and excitement flow down my spine. I felt the book, the author, was speaking right to me. I stood up and went to Jon and we quietly, in our own thoughts, left the garden and its peace, then we entered the maze and the world beyond it.

CHAPTER TEN

There are many ways to arrive at understanding the truth. The truth is a logically undeniable concept. It is something that exists inside of you, which is why so often when trying to recognize the truth of a situation, you get a special understanding of it that radiates from deep within you. When the truth is realized in this way, it cannot be denied, although sometimes we do not want to accept it.

The world is not exactly as it may appear. There are ways of focusing the mind to eternal truths that lead to the improvement of your Self and the world surrounding you. Everyone has the opportunity before them many times in their life to make improvements in these areas. Often life can become lost in circular mazes.

Escaping the circular repressions of life is made almost impossible by the fact that the individual being is raised to embrace and believe in the world that they perceive. Their reality and any efforts to learn the truth of things is, therefore, redirected before they ever really even start. The majority of people are herded throughout their existence to keep the machine of life here going but the end result is constantly benefiting someone else.

Self sacrifice is not the intended course.

Self improvement is the goal.

I sat back for a moment, removing myself from the book, taking in what it was that I had just read.

This unknown author is writing a wild and intricate story but it is about God. It's not religious but definitely a spiritual story about choices and eternal truths that we should all know. It's...almost certainly fiction, something that is rarely thought about, God.

Interesting that it is that way now.

What if… it couldn't be real though, but… what would it be like, to know God's story, the real story?
I seriously bet Lisa would enjoy reading this book.
I think she would love it, I think anyone would.
What am I talking about? I barely know her.
But I am drawn to her like I do know her, I argued with myself. I shook my head to clear my thoughts.

The giant clock on the wall revealed the time to be-
1:01 PM
I can't seem to move forward with reading for an extended moment out of some great concern that green eyes will definitely enjoy this book.
Or is it that I think she might like me and I want a reason to talk to her?
That's probably it…
No… I just really think she will enjoy the book, besides I can tell she likes me.
Unable to contain myself, I leaned toward her and said,
"Hey, if I finish this in time, I think you should take it and check it out. It's pretty good and I just found it sitting here anyways… so …it's not really mine. It's a really cool storyline, about life… choices…

and gods, so far at least, but yeah I think you should check it out...it is about God." I finished quickly slightly embarrassed that I fumbled my words so much.

She smiled and again with a reticent response,

"OK... if you finish that is, there is not much time before we board and it looks like you have a ways to go. That book found you, you have to finish it before it can find its way to someone else."

She smiled again and went back to typing what appeared to be a text message.

I wonder who she is texting?

What? Why am I wondering?

I need to hurry and finish this book.

I will leave my card in the book when I give it to her, so she will have my contact information, then if she so chooses, maybe she will call me or something. I mean, if she's interested she would call... I hope.

Maybe I should ask her for her contact information?

But...she might feel more comfortable if I just give her the option to call if she wants. Yeah... that's what I'll do, give her the option.

Stop thinking about her for a little bit, I scolded myself.

I had better finish the book.

I skipped ahead a bit further to help my goal of getting this book into her hands.

I began flipping and scanning through some future pages

Page 248 caught my attention

Questions and answers

What is love?

Love is a concept discovered by Adonae millions of years ago to help explain his thoughts and feelings toward his fellow creators. The word is a collection of abstract meanings now but love was originally a real feeling seeking a definition, then it became a thought, followed with a real desire for action.

There are hundreds of different types of love and different ways of letting that particular love be expressed. However, the full ramifications of the concept came into existence more than sixteen thousand years after Adonae realized himself out of the mist. It happened when the god, Elizabeth, realized herself into existence.

It has been speculated by some gods that Adonae and Elizabeth were somehow linked inside the mist and have always been eternally infinite in all directions. They are the cause of everything. It is their love that saves, protects, and creates eternity constantly.

It is known by many that Adonae developed a working conceptualization of love to better explain the way he felt about Elizabeth; a new type of love he felt after she became. Adonae loves to have the opportunity to explain his belief, that they were opposing magnetic forces that attracted each other's energy, that once they were attracted, they flow in harmony creating love and peace, infinity in eternity.

Most believe the eternal connection between Adonae and Elizabeth cannot be broken. This idea has been true for many, many others as well. There are many connections. In one word it was described as soulmates. Although Adonae did not come up with the term, he does love to use it. He believes each is a whole being but half of a greater whole, woven together in such intricate design that when reunited is an unbreakable bond, a beautiful thread stronger and more consistent than the pull of gravity itself.

Love is an eternal Truth.

Before I could finish the page, in bold letters at the bottom of the next page, three words caught my eye and I realized I didn't really know the answer to the question.

What is virtue?

So, of course, I eagerly turned the page to find the answer.

Virtue is to be morally excellent. Simply put-to be good always. A virtuous being is exceptionally accurate at everything, due to consistent proper choices and the development of good habits. Above all, this being has succeeded in developing a good, consistent moral core.

In the eternal realm, this is something all gods have inherently due to proper development. Choices they have made are moral and True and all future decisions will continue to be aligned with the truth. They have different paths within their spectrum and different virtuous qualities that make them who they uniquely are but at their core they are morally excellent.

If they choose to be born as a physical being, the development starts over and can be very complicated to attain their moral excellence again... but not impossible. Once physical, one must be concerned with character development. What is good character?

A possibility we are born with that constantly is developing within us. It is something that can and must be developed properly if it is to be accurately realized. It is courageous and protective, tolerant and compassionate; it has a solid and accurate sense of Truth, always.

If one can develop these traits, they will have an easier time of recognizing and consistently making the right decisions and knowing quickly what course of action to take in any situation. You will need to improve areas if your foundation is to become solid.

If you do not already have all of these traits- study them and learn them. You can become the person you want to be. Your actions define who you ultimately are. Look at every moment as a new moment to implement what you have learned.

You are constantly Becoming.

People have the ability to develop these traits but it will take time, therefore, patience, understanding and above all consistency is an absolute necessity. You must stay consistently mindful in order to achieve the fullest possibilities of your being.

Consistency.

Good character must translate into choices, actions and conduct.

You are who you act like you are.

Who we choose to be-
is who we are

I hope all of this helps!

~*~

I haven't felt like writing much lately. I've been going through some sort of transition. I think I am still in the middle of one…it is getting easier though. So often I feel like I can control my feelings so well, when all that I am really doing, I think, is blocking my emotions, there is just so much going on.

This is such a complicated creation, this life. I've been really confused lately about how best to proceed and for a while I didn't think I was anymore. I guess that is how confused I've been! I know what I want and where I'm going for once and I guess that's what is confusing for me because I am constantly drawn to solutions for everyone else's problems. I became so used to living for the Now, not being at all concerned with the future. I now realize there must be a balance among the current moments, the past, and all of the tomorrows that are coming.

My thinking, my views, are clearer now. I'm calm and organized but I haven't allowed myself to be truly happy for awhile. I've just pushed all my feelings and others away. I have been so busy trying to figure this all out, I have lost some compassion for other people. However, I think I must refocus and get it back because all that I have learned and gained through this has been extremely valuable to my future and where my life is going. I know what my feelings and thoughts are on most things. Now I more fully recognize the complexities and know what they are and what they mean.

Someday I hope to find people happy again, instead of this unsatisfied world. I know that I control my future but I want to help others figure out that they control theirs. I think it might get better if they believed this.

Sometimes I wonder about other peoples' lives. Are theirs getting better?

What are they doing to make it better themselves?

Who are they really?

Are they happy?

We are all apparently different, yet I have discovered that we are similar in more ways than we are different. We are all looking, searching for something more. We all want to love and be loved. We are in relationships because we believe, whether we admit it or not, that there is one person for us in this world. One person who is a perfect match, not necessarily a perfect person but a perfect match for our soul- our soulmate.

Most of the time all we are trying to do is find that person who we feel completes us. The person we get to be who we really are with. It took me a long time to realize that it is me that I have to be comfortable with before I can be my true self with someone else.

It is loving yourself.

Learning how to actually and actively love yourself!

Do that first and you will find the person you are meant to be with. And when you do, you will actually be ready for them.

Ready to love them the way you should.

Remember, you cannot truly love another being if you do not love yourself first.

There are some things you just know.

Why or how you know them are concepts that for so many people seem to remain unsolved mysteries, for lifetimes.

115

Unlocking the mind is a complicated process. I have been blessed with beings and experiences that have helped me grow and understand the Truth.

Almost uncontrollably, I turned ahead a few pages and found another hand written sentence followed by a very interesting opening statement. *How many people have written in this book?* I wondered to myself as I continue to read.

CHAPTER ELEVEN

"The beginning is complex and unique."

With a laugh, he replied, "GOD LANDED IN ARIZONA?"

"Exactly and I don't mean that in any ridiculous or untruthful way. I mean literally landed in Arizona. Once you understand, well, it will make more sense." I pulled it out and gave it to him,
"Take this…it's yours."

Eyes looked at me with genuine confusion.
I cleared my throat, then said, "I believe this will help your understanding process."

He took the book from my waiting hands, turning it over and over again. Watching his hands run over that spectacularly old book, the leather crackling just the slightest, was soothing and familiar. I could feel the excitement flowing through me.

I was so exhilarated!

I had found him!

He had found this moment!

It is so peaceful, at this instant, knowing that once he has read what is within the leather his hands are still exploring, he should understand.

He opened the book and began to read-

I am going to tell you a story.
The story is going to make you cry...
Do you remember this?

Can you remember this?

There was a mist that hovered effortlessly, peacefully, and forcefully in all directions of eternity. This primordial mist contained everything and at the same time contained nothing yet it contained all potentiality.

More than thirty billion years ago, out of a primordial mist- I realized My Self and actualized my being into existence.

I remember my thoughts as I realized I have already experienced everything but I did not have direct immediate access to the memories and knowledge I gained throughout the experiences.

I did not come into existence.

I existed.

I was aware of the reality that I was realizing my experience.

I realized I was.

I looked upon the mist that I had come from-I remember being there, being complete and whole, in a blissful yet curious state. But now I was looking upon it from above. Nothing else was in existence...

...Just the mist and I.

My thoughts were fast and clear. I was taking in so much new information, yet I still had some memories from within the mist.

I had a thought that lingered in my mind about what would come out of the mist next. A flood of questions ran through me-

Would anything come out?

Why did I come out?

Am I here for a reason or a purpose?

This promoted many fundamental thoughts to dominate my being.

How did I come out of the mist?

Who was I?

What am I now?

Am I the same thing as before?

Why are my memories from within the mist incomplete?

I felt different.
Do I look different?

What do I look like?

As I thought of these questions, I realized that whoever or whatever I am, I for certain exist, here right now. I am aware of that.

I am aware that I am aware but what exactly am I aware of?

What is this place?

With only myself and this mist...

...I considered going back in... but why I am here, there must be a reason I am certain.

122

I easily realized, from somewhere inside my being, that I truly desired to wait a little while and see what happened next. This experience was something spectacular.

Everything was so astounding, yet so fantastic!

The more that I was there, the more I thought about, and the more I realized I could think about. There was so much to experience and realize, things that I am now certain can only be accurately understood by experiencing them. It quickly occurred to me that I must record, in some manner, what I was thinking and feeling.

As I read, I got the image of there being black, dark nothingness but a man sitting at an old wood desk, so involved in his thoughts and feelings. I read on:

Time flows by so quickly-
I have begun to feel the information building up within me, like a pressure that needs to be released. This pressure has been released some through writing but I still need to do more. I desire a spoken word record as well, a

verbal story. This needs to be shared with someone else-how exciting it will be to have a conversation with another.

I knew somewhere in the depths of my being that these moments experienced would be the first cause of a whole new something.

This is the beginning.

I have begun to record everything in what I call Histories- different categories for all the diverse areas of my experience. I will hold the writing in this journal special forever and as a place that I can record my free-flowing thoughts.

My Histories, will be technical and instructional but I feel deeply that I need my private thoughts to be separate. I hope that one day I will have the opportunity to share those thoughts with another individual, along with all of my experiences. I am so eager to teach all that I am learning about to someone else. I feel that until the time comes that I can give a verbal account of what I have learned to others, I will not fully understand what is happening.

However, I will continue to enjoy this with these deep feelings, best described as joy and amazement, I will record what it is that I feel, experience, learn, and do.

This truly is amazing, raw and beautiful everywhere I look.

My anticipation of who would come out of the mist next has quickly turned to a vague interest.

There is so much to do!

-I can do whatever I want. Whatever I think about creating in my mind can happen! All sorts of things are being created. As I am recording all of this in my history records, I am continuing to realize that my written words cannot fully describe what I see because of what I feel. This tells me that words have limits. I can write them down but they are nothing compared to what it is that I can see and touch...experience. The true nature of the being needs to be experienced in order to understand.

I wish that I had someone to show all of this to.

-After a while, I have begun to entertain the idea that no one might come out. I have to ponder the fact that I may be alone here for a long, long time.

-Today I began creating and shaping the corners of what I have decided to call the figure. So when I show those whom may come out next, the realities I have realized, there will be a defined space to realize those realities We all should have the ability to create.

-It is so easy! It truly appears there is nothing that I cannot do. I am learning more about what powers I have every moment. I have yet to think of something that cannot be created. I can go anywhere I want and do what I want with just my mind. My mind appears to be limitless in power outside of the mist.

- I was moved with the thought that I was creating this all on a tremendously grand and vast stage; a stage that appears to continue on infinitely in all directions with so many things possible, so many things to discover and learn about. This is Life-full and everlasting.

To more blissfully spend my time, I have created numerous systems, systems that are the building blocks to something else, throughout the various corners of the figure.

With all of this power, I have quickly realized that the true and eternal feeling of compassion is an essential and necessary attribute. As I have learned to release the pressure of knowledge and experience through my written words, I have found a new pressure building inside of me.

This force, I believe, comes from my Absolute attachment for all that I create. I feel compassion; I feel an exciting amount of compassion for everything that I make. Through all of my experiences I feel compassion in several ways: Truth, understanding, love. I feel connected to *everything. From the depths of my being I know this word* *love. All that I am creating, I feel so pleased.*

-Note to Self: It turns out that creating things that *will be self-sufficient is a very delicate process. Remember* *always that this process cannot be rushed. It takes another* *trait that I discovered... patience. With patience and* *compassion, combined with time, I can produce countless* *extraordinary things.*

Today it worked-I have created my first planetary system that works together with a central, self-sustaining power source, which I call the Astar. There are animated, orbiting bodies, whose existence stays intact as long as the energy source reaches them. I have considered the possibility of this continuing to exist indefinitely.

The bodies in this system necessarily require the energy given from the power source to survive as well as to stay in the correct orbit. But as I have found, the source cannot be too close, nor can it be too far, it must be the exact, perfect range.

It was incredible to watch the moment the bodies took arrangement and fell into a perfect, beautiful orbit. It was truly spectacular!

It appears that this system required my mind only to create and begin its life cycle. Now it is existing even when I am not thinking of it. The piece I was missing before, with the ones that failed to survive, was trying too hard to be perfect; what I needed to do was step back a bit and realize there is a range I must align the processes with and then let the rest unfold before me. I think I can only start the process; I cannot make alterations once it has begun.

129

It seems that you either get the range correct from the start with all of the bodies falling into their place in an orbit, or you get it wrong, things get very dark and everything within the system fails rather quickly. My interactions before, trying to fix areas I saw failing, appeared to speed up a collapse of the system. With my latest creation I was patient and observed, even when I thought it was failing. I just watched and trusted I had understood the range and created it correctly.

It worked-the system has been self-sustaining for a while now, orbiting and evolving perfectly. This is my first perfect system of evolving life.

I love it!

It is magnificent!

-Today I discovered within my creation, a very fast evolving planet within my system. I began observing many parts of it. I believe someday this will be a unique and complex paradise that will be big enough for me to interact with it on some levels without causing its collapse. This beautiful place will be for others to come visit; a place to admire and enjoy. It will be the foundation for what we can create; combining all of my discoveries- patience, compassion, love and evolution into this one planet-it will be a paradise.

~ Drifter's Paradise ~

So much time has gone by, eagerly awaiting the arrival of a friend. Last night I realized that I did not know exactly how long, how much time I had been creating here. So I decided to create a system for marking time, so I will know exactly how long events take to occur, created as a new thought to describe my life and my perspective on what is unfolding here.

It seems important to have an accurate way to record the concept of time, because it is happening, it is becoming something. The words seem to make themselves, as if that is what they are and what they have always been and what they will always be; Words like time, love, patience, understanding and Truth. They are what they are and what they will always be.

This makes me wonder what came before me, what created the mist and me? I feel the answer, deep within myself.

"You are Adonae-you are the beginning of this experience and you will always be a part of it, the middle, and the end. You were the mist and now everything that comes out of it is… a part of you. Everything you create is a piece of you. There is no teacher for you, you are the Teacher. The untaught will be the one to teach what all others will be taught."

131

- I created plant life which comes from seeds I collected from the edges of the mist. I let it blow into the soil that is abundant and rich, eager to grow life, in many areas on my paradise. I discovered seeds need several things to grow: water, which seems to be a necessity for most living things that exist, and some kind of consistent energy source. I had tried and failed with so many sources, all of them failing rapidly. This one has worked, the Astar; it too struggled to get started but now appears to be accurately feeding. I think I will be spending a lot of my time developing more ideas here. So far the development is astounding!

I love this place!

-So much life is everywhere, in so many varieties-this place is a growing paradise. I am so excited now after learning that I actually can interact with this place without any apparent negative consequences, I have decided to commit to perfecting and enjoying every detail.

-I have been very busy since I first experienced Drifter's Paradise. My histories are increasing rapidly.

Today, all day again, I walked throughout paradise, touching, smelling, and enjoying the many amazing and intricate life parts that are developing. Everything is growing. There is even new growth connecting and interweaving without my help. It is as if Drifter's has come to life and is growing on its own. It doesn't seem dependent on me for its creations I thought it and created what I saw and now it survives independent of me. I believe we are linked in some manner but we are physically separate. I still feel eternally and emotionally connected to this creation.

Through these life forms I grow and gain more knowledge. While my existence is not contingent on them, they do have an affect on me, a brilliant and incredible affect. I am humbled by this experience that is unfolding before me.

·-As time has passed I have noticed an evolution of many of my creations. The reality that has become of all creation, is that what is created is not stagnate; reality progresses forward, resulting in creation constantly growing, developing, and becoming something more. Something thriving, beautiful and strong, sometimes very different from what it started out as.

-What an amazing day! I had almost forgotten about my hopes of being able to teach others and show others who we are and what we can create.

-Today another realized himself out of the Mist. He looked just as I might have looked years ago. I am so excited-I felt as if I could explode in all directions!

We spoke for a long time and I answered many questions. I immediately began showing him all that I have created. I showed him that he has the same abilities that I have. The creativity comes with time and practice. It is taking him some time to understand the 'why' in what I am trying to teach him but he is so young yet. I think he has eternal time and experiences, as do I.

Mine is felt as memories, I wonder if he is the same?

This is marvelous!

I gave him the name Jon. The name came to me easily and I realized this has probably always been his name just as mine, I remember, has always been Adonae. I am keeping so many written and precise records of all that I am discovering. I truly cherish the moments of free-flowing dialogue that I have with Jon.

My inner thoughts in this book will always be special and important. I already spoke to Jon about writing; I showed him how and encouraged him to do it often. I think he will. He seems eager to be with me as do I with him. I often notice him staring deeply at things. I remember when the vastness would pull at me the same way. The feeling of experiencing with another is even more fulfilling than I had imagined it to be.

Today I realized-
All things created will progressively travel through the
Space time of this
Eternal abyss-before my eyes,
I exist within this wonderful, eternal abyss.

"Is this for real, Jon? Are you the same Jon as Adonae was describing? The second one out of the mist?"

"Why do you think I am that Jon? Is it because I have the same name?"

"Hmmm?" was all I could say. Maybe I do think that he is the Jon because of the name. But it is something more that makes me feel that way, kind of like how the truth feels when it is spoken. It is definitely something to think about though, considering one of our previous conversations also made me think that.

You are not who you think you are... whispered a voice.
The words floated, strange and unfamiliar, at me from nowhere but still coming at me somehow and for all of my mind.

What is this??
Why is this??
...Wait!

Jon started speaking again. A sense of peace washed over me and I sat down in a chair, leaning in deep to hear the words better.

"It is important for you to know that all of what you know did have a beginning. There was *the first being to begin to gather knowledge and learn the eternal Truths. He exists; has always existed. He created everything that is known by the human mind. You will learn this Truth. You will learn, just as I did, that all things created, grow in a balance. It is the reality of this balance that has created the fate of this world."*

"I believe once you have read the pages in that book you will understand your life and your world in a new, true, pure and moral manner. The "idea" of the many godlike beings that every civilization has worshipped in some manner is not false.

The idea is tangible, authentic and True because God does exist and wants desperately to help you experience the Truth and get back to the eternal reality you were a part of. He wants this because until you realize the Truth, you will continue to believe that you are less than you are.

Once you have realized the Truth, you will feel liberated from thoughts that are dominating and distracting your daily life world. You will feel free, clean, pure, moral, powerful, and above all, knowledgeable. The truth will kindly elevate you to a level of understanding that promotes your fullest potential."

"As you continue to grow, you must learn to accept that there is not a way around the

continual influx of spectacularly good and dreadfully bad experiences in this world. It is simply put: an eternal fact of the flow.
Stay focused.

Develop and maintain your mental, emotional and spiritual strength. They also are real and on a spectrum, therefore you can improve and even perfect them. The ability to have faith in the Self and the ability to love with compassion is the quickest and most fulfilling path to true enlightenment. It is certain you will need to become mindfully self aware on a level much higher than you are on now if you are to fully understand.

"There is a tremendous strain on the mind for all beings that are here. The mind is where ALL experiences meet then reside. I promise to only allow you to learn the truth from me. The world is constantly changing-constantly in a state of flux. This roller coaster ride effect will make it difficult to stay focused and not get distracted.

Changing faces…

…Changing places…

…and changing pseudo-truths

It's all changing!

You are also changing, growing, developing because you are Becoming something more than you currently are. Do you feel it?"

"What am I Becoming? What is that? Is it good?"

"Of course it is 'good' because 'good' is a term for <u>true</u>. You have asked many questions throughout your life and you strongly desire answers to the biggest most profound questions out there. These answers can become known to you."

"You have been searching all your life for some ultimate, eternal truth. An eternal truth that until now, you were not one hundred percent sure actually existed but you always believed that it did. Now you have enough of the pieces put together that you are starting to see there is a pattern. With each new piece of knowledge, your desire increases. The whole picture is nearly complete for you, but not just yet. A little more time is needed.

I sense the love that has grown inside of you as you have been putting all of this together. I see how close you are."

"Just being alive makes me happy," I said, almost giddy. "There is so much here to

see, to experience, and to learn. It is…..beyond words. I can't say that I have always felt this way though. I had to choose it. I have gone through too many things in my life that I could have allowed myself to stay stuck in that mess."

That is what I think I find the most frustrating about people. They all have a choice to be happy no matter the life they have lived up until that moment and so many of them choose to blame something or someone else, even God. Sometimes they do this instead of realizing a difficult truth and that truth is that the person responsible for their happiness is themselves.

They are the only person who should be responsible; these are feelings that exist inside of the individual. Each one can choose who they want to be and how they want to feel in every moment.

"Well, Tristin, right there is the key- choice; in every moment. It's always about choice. And you are right; we are all responsible for our own happiness, with no one to blame but ourselves, if we are not happy.

The choices exist in abundance every moment of life. The choices made from one moment to the next are what shape the parameters of the individual futures. If you're not happy, do whatever it takes, even if you have to walk to where you are happy."

141

"Do you recall taking your college placement tests?" he asked, switching tracks completely and throwing me slightly off.

"Sure."

"You were nervous, I'm sure?

I nodded, trying to figure out where this was going.

"You were scared you would fail. Yet you chose to take them and go to college, even though no one had ever gone to college from your family before? You broke through a barrier that was placed in front of you."

"What about the three times you took an I.Q. test? You were labeled as someone special long ago, before any of that, but you still did not believe it. Each time you were scared that you had done the test wrong yet still you took them. You knew something was unique about all of this"

I nodded in agreement, slightly stunned about how he knew about that period in my life but let him continue.

"Although you were noticed as smart and you thoroughly enjoyed college, you have never chosen to search the limits of the academic path. Instead, you have chosen to search out the limits of knowledge available from experiencing this world and from studying other's behavior from a distance, a safe way to know someone. You were *interested in learning about an eternal truth that existed and connected all things. You forgot to allow yourself to be open with another soul and that is what has you trapped.*

You have always been more comfortable observing others from a distance, you have been an outlier. Being an outlier has helped foster social inadequacies but people are drawn to you, once they meet you. You radiate the knowledgeable confidence in knowing what is right. Although you have felt inadequate, it never stopped you from wanting to learn more about yourself and the world around you. Do you ever wonder why people are so drawn to you, why so many people want to be around you?"

"Well, I'm not really sure…I guess if they do really feel that way about me it is because I am a good person, a kind and truthful person. But I don't really think about how other people feel about me. I am Me."

"This is true, you are these things but it is also more than that. I want to tell you about someone I once knew…."

"Over the course of time, he has helped me to realize and experience many magnificent and remarkable things. It is not easy going through the life processes. Allowing one's self the opportunities that come from experiencing the procession. In understanding the importance of

taking the time, which results in truly being aware of who you are.

He helped me to learn truths about this world and my Self; many truths that I have strived to recognize throughout time. He taught me how to understand that everything that "is" possible can be learned and created. He taught me about the eternal certainty that states undeniably 'the truth is what the truth is' at any moment... at any time. This level of awareness can take quite some time to attain. As simple as it seems to be, very few get a true appreciation for it but nonetheless-it is.

He taught how easy it is for us to know something partially but we do not truly 'get it' until we have realized it at our core, in our soul. Usually this can only come from personal experience, tremendous self awareness and time but it does not necessarily have to... it is not a given.

"The events that have unfolded and the tales that have penetrated the mind are the result of a long and glorious adventure that is culminating in a revitalization of the soul for the most important being."

Jon paused for a moment, taking a few, what I call reflective breaths, allowing his truths adequate time to sink into me.

This is the ultimate adventure called Your <u>Life</u>!
<u>It</u> is best for you if it is actively and accurately
enjoyed!
<u>This</u> exists in every single right now!

A few minutes passed before Jon began speaking again, the same sense of peace falling over me.

"So much of it is lost when we are born."

"So, what is this right now?" I asked, curiously.

"This is actually a beginning."

"But not the absolute beginning."

"This is a possible beginning of your enlightened experience here but not the beginning of You. When we are born it is because we made a choice to be born here, for the experience usually but sometimes maybe it is to help.

Our eternal consciousness cannot exist in physical form unless we have been born here," his arms stretched outward to display the world, *"and remember, then realize who you are, only then will you find your way home, where we belong. You will then gain the ultimate reality, the ability to come and go spiritually and physically as you please...with no fear of becoming lost.*

However, the realizations necessary to accomplish this are extremely difficult and have become very rare in the current times."
He took a deep breath and then continued,

"I want to tell you that I am speaking logically and with a fully functioning and rational mind when passing on this knowledge that has been taught to me.

The possible world, alpha, is this world you are in now. This alpha world necessarily had a first being. A first creator discovered long ago the realities and possibilities that necessarily exist within eternity and here. He is here now on this planet, living a life similar to your own.

Take from your life lessons what you need to find your way, become balanced and centered, so that in your life right now, you can realize the Truth. Many may choose not to become enlightened and some may rarely if ever have the opportunity to understand what it means. If this is the case, they will be lost for a long time.

I want every human being to have the Truth cross their path and at least have the opportunity to recognize it as the Truth. Once recognized and understood, it is impossible and completely unnecessary to deny.

Change your mind and you change your life forever.

You will understand why you are really here and how best to be. Then become the best you can be, perfect at who you are."

"How do I know the Truth that I see is the correct one?"

"What do you think about the fact that your God is here right now, somewhere on this planet? He is living a life not all that different from yours.
"Understand this truth!"
"He is not here preaching and claiming to be anything other than a good man, an honest man who wants as many people as possible to understand their true and eternal potential. He wants people to be happy and enjoy their life, no matter what they have to go through because they will know the Truth.

All it takes is making the choice to be happy in every moment. The human mind cannot easily absorb the eternal truths that exist. Know that it is possible to be happy in every moment, accept it and enjoy your life."

"I want to help him and you both but I have learned the hard way, just as he has, that a quiet life under the religious and political radar is the best way to be here for a long time.

So we cannot go shouting from mountain tops or start making appearances on Fox or CNN but we can be the pebble thrown into the calm waters of the pond of time and create beauty again. Peaceful ripples of change can work.

These ripples can have a profound, long-lasting impact that can lead to a world of peace and happiness throughout time. This possibility exists and we understand that words focus the mind. It can allow the ripples of truth and enlightenment to spread to all minds. This combined attention can change this world or any world."

This is truly the only way that we will be able to get this message to as many people as possible. I chose this path again with only the hope that it will work and no clue where to find him. His message needs to accurately be given to all people; that it will help educate the misinformed and lost masses to change their minds.

If his words have found you and they have, if they made an impact in your mind, then there is a reason for that. Please, do not turn away from this opportunity to more fully develop your eternal soul.

Matthew D. Harding

CHAPTER TWELVE

Three days later…

Tristin and I sat, lost in thought on a sandy beach, the sound of the surf slamming into the rocks that surrounded the cove. The day was slightly overcast but the air was wonderful, a slight chill with a chill from the ocean breeze. The salty smell of the ocean filled our lungs with the cool moist air. I swam my hands through the sand, picking it up and shifting it through my fingers, feeling the primordial energy flow through it as the grains of time fell into a pile.

I looked over at Tristin and watched as he clapped his hands together and then let them *wander across the surface of the book, as he had done many times now. He started to let pages slip through his fingers, his eyes telling me that he was deep in thought, his mind racing, processing all that was coming at him. He took a deep breath and looked out at the ocean. He closed his eyes and let the forceful calming sound of the waves overtake him, relax him. Then, he opened his eyes and slid his fingers over the pages.*

He stopped suddenly, somewhere in the middle of the book and flipped open to a specific page. I glanced over and noticed where he had stopped; I knew this would be beneficial. Energized, as he began reading, I knew that he would have many questions stirring inside him after reading this page. I turned my attention back to the ocean, smiling for the world, as he continued on his journey of knowledge...

The passage was immediately familiar to him...

My first, real conversation here occurred on a beautiful spring afternoon while sitting on the lush, green grass of the brilliantly colored Ricks College campus in Rexburg, Idaho. The air was filled with the scent of lavender.

My legs were stretched out and my head lifted to feel the effects of the sun on my face. I could feel the astounding strength of it radiating throughout my entire body. It was a surreal experience, as if I were experiencing this moment from within a stunningly vibrant piece of art, filled with all shades of green, lush grass and splashes of violet, and large, beautiful trees for a background. Pleasing to the eye.

As I panned my head from side to side, I knew something amazing was about to occur. I could feel it in my soul, energy was eager to be released.

Moments later, I watched as a curiously interesting and naturally beautiful woman walked across the common area where I was sitting. She was familiar somehow, as if I had seen her before but I could not remember the place.

She walked intently across the lawn to a tree that was evidently familiar to her. Sitting down under its branches, she pulled out a book and began to read.

I could picture her being here, under that tree, every school day. That this was a place she felt comfortable and relaxed.

She looked up and her eyes connected with mine for a split second, as if she could feel me watching her. She smiled and then quickly looked down.

Those eyes made my heart skip several beats.

I know her from somewhere.

I could feel her energy flow; it wove itself perfectly into the exquisite scene that I had already begun to paint. She was the center of it, what completed it. I was drawn to speak to her; I knew that I must know her. I needed to look into her eyes, up close, to know what she knew and what she thought of her Experience. Immediately I became aware of a desire in my soul that was compelling me to absorb this unique woman's energy; I needed to experience her energy.

Why? I asked myself.

Why were these feelings happening?

What did they mean?

I had never felt this about another person's energy. I was pulsating with excitement as I boldly rose to my feet, with the sun in my eyes, forcing me to squint as I closed the twenty yards that separated us. With each of my steps, the nervous excitement that had been swirling inside me grew and turned into a comfortable confidence, knowing that not only was I about to speak to her, I was about to know her.

I know this Tristin thought to himself *I know how this is going to end.* But he couldn't stop himself from continuing to read, as though to confirm what he already knew.

As I sat down in front of her, she looked up peacefully, smiled at me, and shyly said, "Hello."
Quickly looking down and guiding her hair behind her left ear.
I replied simply and with a gentle smile,

"Hi." This caused her to look up again, now softly pulling the curls of hair that were resting on her shoulders.
I looked deep into her inquisitive green eyes and asked,
"Are you glad to be here?"

She replied happily and with a little laugh probably wondering who this weirdo was,
"Yeah…I like it here a lot! It is my absolute favorite spot on the campus."

"What about here, this life, this experience- are you glad to be You?"

"Umm"…she smiled so perfectly and looked me in the eye, bit her bottom lip and softly replied- "yeah…yes I am.

This simple exchange of words began my most favorite and memorable discovery.

We began with our reasons for being right where we were at that moment. She was here almost every day, reading, writing, taking pictures, whatever it was that she felt like doing. We then flowed in to what we were doing at that school and before either one of us knew it we were sharing stories of our lives and places we wanted to travel and the dreams of our souls.

I was fascinated with every word that she spoke. I could visualize what she was saying and what she was thinking. We sat there for hours, talking about everything that came to our minds.

It was a very enlightening and stimulating experience. I did not want the moment to end but as with all things, it eventually did. Our good-bye was simple, easy, both of us confidently knowing that we would see each other again, when the time was right. I knew where I could find her and for some reason there was no doubt in my mind that she could find me if she wanted to.

"I hope to see you again soon," she said, smiling at me, playing with her hair again.

I smiled back and nodded my head in agreement, then I turned and walked away.

I stopped suddenly, realizing something and turned back to look at her. She had already started walking away as well but turned to me as if she had known that I had stopped.

It suddenly it occurred to me that we had not exchanged our names at any point during our conversation.

"What's your name?" I called to her, a hint of shyness still in my person.

"Elizabeth,"

She called back with a giggle, probably realizing how silly it was to have just talked to someone for so long and so intently and not have mentioned names,

"What's yours?"

"Tristin."

I quickly darted my eyes up to look at Jon, wanting answers, needing them but Jon was not there. I noticed him a few hundred yards down the beach, hands in his pockets, walking peacefully.

He knew I was reading this part. He had to know I would recognize my own life experience.

I went back to the book to finish the passage before I went to Jon to find the answer to my question.

Walking back to me and extending her hand she said,
"Nice to meet you, Tristin."

> *As our hands slid comfortably into a handshake, our energies were ecstatic at the opportunity to physically meet. I wanted to know her more than I have ever wanted anything or anyone in my entire life.*

> *She smiled at me again, turned and walked away.*

> *As I walked across the campus that day I spoke to my Self in complete amazement, yet pure astonishment to the fact that I now knew for sure that everything was as it was supposed to be. Now I knew why I had traveled so far to go to this school. I knew I would see her again, I knew she was something like me-maybe she doesn't know it yet and if not, she can.*

> *Suddenly, it occurred to me that I would teach her what I had experienced and what I know and she would surely teach me something that I would need.*

I had never before been able to look into another person's eyes and see what I did in her eyes. To feel what her energy allowed me to experience today. I knew it was something unique but I did not yet fully understand the exact meaning of it.

What I knew was the Truth in her eyes and I saw it in her soul and I felt it in her touch.

What an amazing and unexpected discovery!

I knew that I loved her!

I closed the book, so much racing through my mind. Taking a deep, cleansing breath I got to my feet and lightly jogged down to where Jon stood, snapping pictures. *When did he get the camera? Never mind, not the point.* "Where did you get that?" I demanded.

"Best Buy," he replied, slowly bringing the camera down from his eyes and turning to look at me.

"No, not the camera! You know what! You know what I was reading. That was a written description of an event that occurred in my life! I experienced that! How did you know of it, word for word how I thought it and felt it, and how did it get in that book?" I fired at him.

He stared at me for a long moment before he spoke,

"What makes you think that I would know how it got there? If that is your experience, that is your experience, not mine. How would I have anything to do with it? Do you not remember writing it?"

"What? -What am I supposed to do with that?" I asked frustrated, not knowing what else I could say. "I am sure that was my experience, completely. And no I do not remember writing it but that is exactly what I felt and what I thought and what she said and everything! You're telling me that it just magically ended up in this book?"

"No, I am telling you that I have no idea how it ended up in that book. I didn't write that book, I just gave it to you. Maybe someone else happened to have the same experience?"

"Well, then, maybe it's time you tell me who did write that book," I challenged Jon, my arms folded over my chest.

"I already told you. Someone I knew wrote it and gave it to me to give to you. I don't know how or why he put what he did in there but it is all for you.

It is important that you know that I would never lie to you. I may not be able to tell you everything on your time. When you want to know or feel something you should try to achieve that goal with all of who you are. When the time is right you will know.

There are greater things at work here than you can possibly comprehend. Right now trust that it is probably not the time for you to have full knowledge. When it is, everything will make sense and you will hold the answers to the questions that you have sought."

He gave me a smile signaling the end of our conversation. He turned and took one last picture before walking further down the beach, leaving me standing there, staring at a book that held more questions than answers.

I sighed, realizing that what he spoke was true, although my mind could not stop questioning how it got there. I couldn't figure out how anyone could have put my experience with Her in there; with our words and thoughts along with my actions and feelings.

I walked back to where I had left the book. Flopping down on the sand once more, feeling more confused than ever, I picked up the book, flipped to a section I had not yet examined and dove back into the journey.

CHAPTER THIRTEEN

Part 2

Philosophy

I remember my first college philosophy course requesting that we ask ourselves the big questions, questions like-

Is there a God?

Who am I?

Why am I here?

Is there a purpose to my existence?

These questions took me, personally, on an infinite and enlightening journey. These questions were questions that had dominated my mind for as long as I could remember. I was eager to be a part of an organized and instructed effort to answer them.

All of us should have solid, well considered answers to any of the big questions. Personal answers may vary; these differences should be openly and creatively debated.

Why this is began to become clearer one day when a question was posed by my professor,
"Have you ever thought about the concept of possible worlds?"

It meant that any world could be analyzed to determine its possible truths. Philosophy explains that what necessarily follows is that any "possible" world is–possible.

Do I understand what the question means?
–if it is logically possible to exist-then it *is possible, it can happen.*

There are an infinite number of possible future events to choose from. If they are possible, I can choose to actualize any of them in my world.

Everything we do contributes to the possible current, future, and past state of affairs. We create them by choosing. Out of all the possible futures, we choose the one that we have, continuously.

Philosophy then led me to the 'Discovery of Self' idea. It is critically significant how to achieve this level of enlightenment.

How do I become enlightened?

Shouldn't big questions be asked by every person?

Find the answers.

Make it important-

   and do it now.

Everyone should experience a dark, black sky filled with stars in infinite directions. This gives a spectacularly small yet fascinating snapshot of peace. Everyone should view this world from above the atmosphere-the perspective is even more revealing from there.

Stars are things the farthest away from this world-out of all the objects one can see from here. By the time we see the light of their existence, their actual existence is gone, we simply see their remaining light rays traveling to us.

Even with the best of scientific knowledge and with all the known technology and the most powerful magnification machines, we do not definitively know what a star looks like up close, we can only see their radiant effect.

Miraculous

Jon returned from his photographic adventure with the ocean and sat down gently next to me. I stopped reading. Moments passed and we just sat, staring out at the vast ocean, with its setting sun and all the questions of the world floating around in my head. Peacefully, Jon asked,

"Tristin, did you know that more than ninety-nine percent of what actually exists still cannot be seen or understood by human beings on this planet? This is an amazing element, the flipping of truths. Thought of rarely and by so few that it has become an obscure and forgotten notion."

"This startling point is the same with God. This is why we must think on a very deep and sincere level to understand Truth. There are things that are going to be happening, things that you have the power to understand and what to do with it. But you will need to make the right choice moment after moment, until you find your rhythm, your flow if you will. Every time you make that right choice, your 'flow' gets closer and closer to the center, to all that is good."

I thought about this amazing detail, this familiar point.

"Can I do it?" What if what you are saying is the truth, then what happens once you are perfect?

He didn't answer. After a few moments, I spoke again, remembering something,

"I had a strange dream last night. It was an… incredibly vivid dream. It was as if I were you, looking down upon me. But when you spoke, it was my own voice shouting:

'Whoever you think you are, you need to understand it more. It is more precise and it will feel intense for a long, long time!'

I replied back to you, scared now,

'I know you, you are me.'

You said back, 'I am more than you, I am more than this world.

I am right now…this moment. Believe it!

I know who I am.' I shouted."

I turned to him after this and asked,

"Wow!"

"It was one of those dreams that stick with you for a while. What does it mean? What am I to take from it?"

I looked to his face, his eyes, to see what his thoughts were. At first, all I received was his familiar soft smile that told me I had said something pleasing. He continued to look at me and smile. When he finally spoke, he said, "It sounds like you are on the right path to those answers you have desired, if you're having dreams like that."

Not really satisfied with not only his verbal response but his non-verbal ones as well, I turned back to the setting sun to compose my thoughts and the questions floating around my mind.

Sitting on the edge of the pier, I peacefully enjoyed the moment, waiting for the right opportunity to explain what I had to say. He finally looked away from the ocean and down at the book, a look of composed understanding. He held his hands on the pages as if to draw strength from them and then turned to look at me.

I was silent for a moment, to allow myself a deep breath and to put my thoughts in order, so the words that I spoke were the most understandable.

"There are a great many things, Tristin, which I know about you. You are a very smart young man and you, Tristin, have the potential to be anything you choose to be. I say this with the utmost respect and certainty. I am sure that you have heard that you are special from others all your life but you truly are very special. You are…unique." I paused for a breath and then continued, looking back out over the vastness of the ocean.

Tristin's eyes followed mine, settling on the horizon where the sun was setting.

"Because of this, you must more quickly allow yourself to explore the realms of your potentiality and discover who you fully are. No one should ever miss out on an opportunity to experience this world through the eyes of a being that has truly discovered their Self."

"What I am about to tell you was discovered a long, long time ago but was forgotten and has only been periodically and partially reintroduced. The human experience is very old, much older than most believe or want to believe.

There is one glorious, yet at the same time, seriously unfortunate fact of the experience. It is that coming into human existence costs one their eternal memory. You have to grow up from birth to adulthood before you will be able to realize all of your strengths and weaknesses and be able to utilize them to your advantage, if you are to ever fully know the Truth. It is a very complicated survivor's challenge.

169

The whole story is so large that its entirety cannot easily be comprehended within the human intellect. Those who have truly searched for answers without getting lost or distracted often are able to attain their organized goals. Those people are often overlooked or misunderstood by so many. Goals formed with the mind of a mortal being are certainly not the most reliable of paradigms. So, just hear the words in your mind and if you know them, you can see them more clearly. You can see them come to life for you.

There is so much to know about the human experience, the present reality, and the eternal reality. What they think they know to be "facts" is nothing when compared to what is actually available to be known."

"An ultimate reality has always been searched for but never completely realized by man.

This does not mean that it is unattainable, look at what you have already been able to understand. The experience can be cluttered by so many unnecessary distractions.

Many never even know they should be looking for higher meanings to anything. It is really quite sad how much is wasted and left unused here. Obviously it is difficult yet possible. When I consider how much you have learned this time, I know that you started the process in time for it to be possible for an advancement of your soul. It may take time but we still have that."

"Given all the necessary tools and guides you have realized a great deal while others given all the same tools and guides realize very little. You are special, you are very special."

"What you think you know to be true does not hinge on it being true and believed by man. The Truth is and it will always be that any false is a non-truth. If it is false, it is wrong."

"Life, God, love, morality, compassion, patience are words thought to be chosen or created by man to represent something abstract and unclear, something to be studied or debated but they are in reality, eternal living Truths; that is what they have always been and will always be. You know this to be true."

Part 3
Life

Let's consider life-
When trying to think of this concept
The easiest way is to get Enlightened,
Then...
Think of it like a dream you wake up from
And realize your whole life is in the eternal dream.
The Great Bliss.

CHAPTER FOURTEEN

Seven days later...

This time we found ourselves in a forest, rich in trees. Peace was in the air. We walked quietly through the trees and brush, making our own path, smoothly, so not to disturb too much of our majestic surroundings. In the distance, a deer was rustling through the bushes. Birds were flying from tree to tree, their excitement apparent.

Taking a deep breath, my lungs rapidly filled with fresh pine; we were deep in the forest. We found a clearing with a small stream bordering it on the north side and a boulder that

173

looked like a giant chair carved out of stone. Tristin jumped into the grand chair and settled with his hands behind his head, eyes turned toward the blue sky, the book lying on his stomach; I smiled to myself and lay down on the moist earth.

"Here, let me see the book," I said, "There is something that I want to show you. I think it is important".

As he jumped down, he smiled slyly, then handed me the book. I could see in his eyes that he was somewhat anxious about what was going to be shown to him. I flipped the pages and easily found what I was looking for. As I read the opening lines in my mind, it made me smile and I smiled for Tristin. I placed the book, open to the page, in his waiting hands, pointing to the spot where he was to start and watched as he eagerly took it and began reading.

The mist realized his existence.

Thoughts became reality.
Thoughts are infinite in all directions of eternity at every moment.

As the interacting thoughts create realities with one another, many worlds are created. Thoughts are everywhere, beautiful free floating images of Mind. You can freely choose to play with your world and create a reality that can only be created by <u>you</u>. It is possible for the enlightened ones to intervene into other worlds but it has become dangerous and risky. Originally they were only to do this to teach and to develop. Once evil became known, the distraction and destruction of worlds became possible, fewer came. Choose life, love, and beauty and all things can be wonderfully revealed again.
It is that simple.

∞

I have walked throughout eternity learning endless amounts of knowledge and feeling endless amounts of energy. Discovering along the way there were no clear limits to what could be made or what could be created.

175

One of the greatest gifts realized is Life.

How simply it can occur...

Life was a way to get the other souls out of the mist. The idea was a spectacularly unique idea. Space-time and experience allowed me to figure out how it all works. Souls are being born as babies into a paradise that I created long ago for the experienced to navigate through. Initially, raising infant souls was complicated and time consuming...chaotic.

Although the task was not easy it became simpler through the realization of the skills of organization and consistency. I love all souls very much and it can be a very enjoyable experience. Jon and I raised the entire first generation on our own, as a perfect team. Eventually, there were eight of us teachers. This period of time was so much fun, difficult at times but very rewarding. This team learned the processes that work and they became great teachers of our processes.

I found that watching another teach using these methods was rewarding and gave me a sense of peace and unity for all that would come. They believed and respected what had been given to them. They taught because they loved life, they loved themselves and they loved all those who they helped teach. It was beautiful to be a part of. Peace was everywhere.

I have written many, many books on these experiences and adventures, which have been used for billions and billions of years as guides through the maze of life.

I sat there watching him read, knowing what he was hearing in his mind, looking for some sign that he was enjoying his reading, that it was maybe even making more sense.

Something familiar must have passed through his memory because suddenly he started flipping back through pages he had already read, using his fingers to slide down the page; he was looking for something and it looked like he might know where it was. His eyes scanned page after page. Then he stopped and motionlessly began to read every word again.

I remember the first person who ever truly irritated me; it was during a debate in philosophy class in which I was attempting to prove the existence of a non-perfect God, who has developed into a near perfect being, a first being that learned through trial and error, all the necessary eternal truths then taught these eternal truths to others.

"Why is it necessary that God be perfect?" I had claimed.
The disruptive soul sarcastically threw up the question-
"What religion are you anyway?"

The entire class became hushed. This question had absolutely nothing to do with the discussion...right?

My religion...hmmm?

I studied him with curiosity and eagerness building inside me, I enjoyed giving my response, I hoped I could change his mind-
"Is it not necessarily understood that if God were to buy into a concept of religion, his religion would be above all other forms of religion because it would be of the exact and pure Truth-undistorted or misinterpreted? The Truth He discovered is known and understood. So, I would say that I belong to the religion of God's Truth."

He started flipping through the pages again, this time with a smile. It made sense-it was exactly how he thought. It is not what religion says but what the truth is. Religion just helps some arrive there. As he flipped backwards through the book, something caught his eye and he stopped again.

16.787 years passed before my beloved Elizabeth came and I have spent the last 30.400,857,028 years since that day loving, learning, exploring and creating with her.

I began writing to help myself fully realize, fully become aware of the true existence of potentiality. I discovered the power to understand that potential is an infinite spectrum.

Elizabeth understands this now.

I still love the sound of her name...

*...**Elizabeth.***

I could see the recognition in his face. Her name rang in his heart and the feeling of her filled his soul. I could tell he was still unsure if this was because of his Elizabeth or Adonae's. But questions regarding her would be asked and answered at another time, as he had flipped ahead three pages, to something else that caught his eye.

You want to know why?

You want to know why there is so much evil in this world?

179

Do you really think you want to know?

Yes!!!

Slowly I began-

The problems, falsehoods, negatives, and badness in all reality arose from the discovery that there was another way out of the mist and the fact that life could be created from combining various parts of eternity. The fact that life could be created in multiple ways created confusion. Where there was previously one option, now there was two. It all went wrong due to the lack of education or the inaccurate education of the gods coming into existence.

Some proposed that it was eternity that created and allowed life to be realized. With this eternity, life became a substance. Adonae's method was perfect. It was ordered and precise. The other was risky and unknown. But Adonae was silent.

A choice had to be made.

You could safely encourage a god to be born out of the mist. However, it is easily realized that these souls being born out of the mist do not automatically retain knowledge of all things held inside of the mist. These gods have to grow emotionally as well as spiritually into being true gods. It takes many years to be ready. Raising gods is a very difficult, consuming, and mentally challenging experience. It requires constant focus at the personal level to consistently be the right leader. God status can sometimes take hundreds or even thousands of years to obtain in this world, even with a dedicated teacher. The gods at this entry level have no understanding of current Earth time-reality, as well as having no concept of the thing we have always called Life.

Life is a substance.

When it is born, it is washed clean…a new beginning.

The most difficult of all creations is of course, the substance, Life and all its many forms. The human potentiality aspect of the substance grew so fast it could be argued that it quickly controlled the gods' ambitions for a period of time.

What is it to be a god in human form?

Complicated

Exactly what it is to be human?

There is an eternal soul that is trapped in a body without leaving it, until death comes to the body; generally trapped for a number of years.

All the gods were pure and true upon first realization but it is not that simple. They possessed the same attributes yet many were opposites in balance because they were physically here living their life on the mass formerly known as "Drifter's Paradise". The

181

ability to experience a bodily form that allows them the ability to physically and actively interact with this material world is the gift of this paradise. These opposites grew into equal strengths and struggles for control became reality.

A necessary balance developed in nature between physical and non-physical, which can never fully go away.

One often chooses to fight for control and domination of all things. Instead of simply living and growing into who they are, loving, then evolving their souls to understand certain eternal truths.

There is an idea of good and bad, right and wrong here. There was a time when there was only good...

Truth exists completely, everywhere. The opposites existed and fit together to create a necessary balance. It is eternal; it is available for recognition in every moment, for every being, physical or non-physical forever.

Here I am trying to steer the evolution of this great planet by reconnecting it with its creator. We have beings born as tiny pieces of their previous eternal selves into the ongoing struggle for understanding and balance.

A necessary battle of opposites is now purposely manipulated against the Truth to create a struggle that over many thousands of centuries began to continually work to obscure the eternal existence of the Truth.

The possibility for soul destruction was the birth of evil. Many billions of years had passed with only Truth in existence. In understanding the necessity of the proper balance between right and wrong, I never saw this birth of destruction coming until it was alive and a real possibility, by then it was too late to eliminate. It could from that moment on only be minimized, once realized it existed it has caused the necessary balance to be…terribly out of balance at times.

I have hoped for a long time that if I sent a piece of my own soul to inspire the eternal truths of love, peace and compassion into this world that it would correct itself eventually. Or that some gods that freely chose to be born into the struggle, knowing the possibilities, yet still attempting to restore enough balance would eventually succeed and the earthly reality would return to its proper balanced position.

How quickly time goes by when you are trying to change the reality for the world! If perfect balance can be realized again it could be kept that way indefinitely but little has worked. Yet… I believe that evil has become so powerful and deceptively interwoven into reality that there is only one way to restore the balance. The way is only a possibility but is possible to understand and see how it could work, although it could take several lifetimes.

I will find the way to remember. I will be stuck in a reality that I freely chose to be a part of. It is not a bad thing to experience this world because if you are alive and have a physical body- you chose to be there, you chose to do something. Whether it was to help or just the experience of life and got lost. Know that you can get out, you can realize the Truth. It may be difficult; it may take a level of mindfulness that seems impossible, it will take an every moment level of attention on the Truth and constantly making right choices. You choose your destiny.

I have never previously been born as a man into existence. Some have often referred to this in an attempt to discredit me, or show a weakness in me. I am not weak, I am eternal Truth because I exist and have existed in eternity from the beginning. You all exist in this world because of me. I am sorry that I could not personally teach each and every one of you the reality of Truth and answer any of your questions.

I have sent you my soul in so many powerful ways. Yet you still have to call to me for help. I have tried to teach you through so many different voices and forms. Yet you now argue over my existence. How confused you all are! You ask for my help and wonder where I am, then fight to remove the idea of me in every way possible. Whether it be removing prayer in school or hindering the ability and opportunities to teach your children how to be and how to care about others. Maybe it is by taking my name out of your courthouses or off your money. You are trying to forget me!

It was first done by rejecting the thought that I could make a mistake. I have had so much faith in you realizing and following the truth than you have in my existence.

Do you really believe all of this happened by accident?

The Truth is being hidden from you.

I have sent you so many to get the message to you in whatever way that I could and you have sacrificed them all for the possibility to deny the Truth. If you break anything down, if you dissect anything down to nothing what you have is nothing. That is it.

The answers you have always searched for are big, not small; the small is for decoration. There is no secret key or magical path to them, just quiet, consistent reflection into your individual Self. Listen to the quiet; enjoy the beauty around you in every moment. These answers are not hidden from you. They are inside, safe and waiting for you to realize them.

Your world's reality hides the possibilities, to control you and this paradise. This truthful realization is difficult to fully grasp at first because it is the created false reality of this world that has taught you to look everywhere else except where the Truth actually is, safe and true inside you.

I will remember.

So I have decided, I will come and speak to you in flesh, as a physical being... a man and see how effective I can be at teaching the world the eternal Truth.
The question is, will you hear me?

I feel that it is time for me to be born into existence; born into your created reality. I will become a physical being and be able to physically and consistently interact, for a lifetime, as a man, on my Drifter's Paradise.

Maybe I am overdue but, nonetheless, I am coming now. This is something that I must accomplish so I can restore the faith necessary for your souls and mine to realize true, whole, eternal existence. The reality has become that you can be lost. I believe that it is possible to be born physically there and be successful at becoming a physical god; even knowing that I will have no recollection of the mist or any of the eternal truths that I know.

I will realize who I am and what I have created, just as I did when I realized my existence from the mist. I have always believed that if you stay focused on the processes developed, all gods born into existence can succeed.

Some have rejoined us but over time fewer and fewer are returning to eternity. Not one has been able to permanently affect the false direction the souls on Drifter's Paradise are going. This tells me that there is something terribly wrong, something that if it is possible to change it, then I must help; I believe I can have a positive impact.

I recently learned there is an evil there that I did not think was possible. Now that I know that it is possible, I must do what I can to eliminate its existence in "time".

Birth is an entrance into the paradise.

Many people realize pieces of the Truth; it impacts many, many lives.

I realize that I eventually will return back with my family of other gods and live life in the happiest, most realized state in eternity.

I come here with the goal of informing as many people as possible that the Truth is real and should be searched for in a very diligent and precise manner. First, know that you are not the body, you are the being inside. You can see it when you are looking in the mirror and it is staring back at you, giving you guidance and strength, answers and more questions to seek answers for.

Look into your own eyes, what do you see?

What do you believe?

However, if I do not figure this out I will have to continue living out my existence as peacefully as I collectively can decide. The possibility does exist that I could remain lost indefinitely, continuously coming back to the physical world and never again gaining access to or existing in the eternal world.

I do not believe that I will allow that to happen. I refuse to accept the possibility that I will get lost. I know that my time there will not be easy, especially with all that is going on and when the force of nature feels the strength of my realized soul, it will make life more challenging for awhile. Obstacles will be in the way, distracting from knowing the truth.

You will know that you want to live, you will desire to exist so much that when you make the journey, you only know of two options: physical existence and non-existence, you all choose so quickly. When there is actually a third option- the right choice- eternal existence.

∞

There are some things that you just know... but how is that?

Why is it that we know them?

The original 'why' and 'how' are concepts that for so many people remain unsolved mysteries. Unlocking the mind is a complicated process. Use your experiences and the people around you to grow and understand the Truth. Start by developing the ability to recognize the truth in any situation you are in. Pay attention.

The ability is inside every single being to learn from the mistakes they have made and see where they erred in their world. The past cannot be changed but the future is up to the individual. They can choose to not make the same mistake, showing the lesson has been learned and hence their experience is better.

You choose your own destiny... no one makes it for you, no one does it but you.

The goal of this world is not the social status you are in or the job that you have but the recognition of your Self and the relationships you have with those around you. Whether they are in your life for a few hours or a few decades. The close ones are drawn

188

to you for a reason; learn all that you can from them. The goal is realizing the Truth in all of this as quickly as possible, so that you can more fully enjoy your time.

∞

CHAPTER FIFTEEN

He looked up at me with a special look in his eye, as if he wanted to say something important, like he had something he had wanted to say for a long time. Without saying a word I took out a pen and handed it to him. He took the pen, settled back on the rock and began writing eagerly in the back of the book. On one of the many blank pages still left…

I almost died many, many years ago. No one knows what really happened but in reality something inside me changed. I tried to forget about it for a long time but have never really been able to fully succeed. I didn't even come back a kid. I came back something a little different, happier and more content, much less angry and a lot more curious about the world.

After that I thought about things the average kid apparently does not think about. I worried about things years ahead of anyone my age. At the time I had no clue as to what was really developing, constantly changing everywhere. Maybe I started to understand too early. I have tried so hard and what I've done is learn to love. I believe

I can become better than who I am right now. As the realization of who I am and what I am is becoming clearer to me I am feeling so many things. I remember so much. Things fit into place, where before the answers had seemed just out of my reach. I feel as though my subconscious knew and was somehow trying to tell me. This is what is happening to me right now.

The hardest part at times has been in the letting go of the negativity that has drifted through my life. While I was trying to figure things out and put them in place, I have had so many distractions coming at me, trying to deter me from my goal. There have been more people in my life that have been lost or wrong for me, then there have been those important to my development. But the good kind way that a few have treated me, left a stronger, more impactful meaning in my life.

It appears to me the problem arises when we fight that battle within ourselves to let go of the bad and live only with the good. So many end up bitter and angry with those who have a negative affect on their life and in return we can take it out on the people closest to us. This can sometimes result in losing those people.

The lesson that I have on this is from the falseness I have felt in my life. I am the one allowing it to be there. Once I recognize it, I must immediately begin a process to remove it. Don't look to assign blame anywhere but inside yourself. How arrogant of someone to think that they could have control over another person's actions and thoughts. The only thing I have control over when it comes to another person is the affect I allow them to have on my life. Yet again it comes down to choice. I think that this happens to everyone.

Given the negativity in the world today, far too many let the illusion of control take power and determine their lives. They allow themselves to believe that another person has control over their life, their feelings, and their thoughts. They believe it is real...which makes it real, to them.

How do we help them see that this is false?

When you are sent somewhere for training, you are not supposed to want to stay. You are supposed to move on, grow, evolve, learn, to become something greater than you were when you arrived. People today just make themselves comfortable here because from birth on, humans are taught to want and how to get what they want. I can imagine that kind of innocence is splendid when you exist on a higher plane but for humans it is manipulated and controlled by the dark clutter.

This is a training world!

We're not meant to stay here.

Very few realize that they already know it. They just need to remember.

When you understand it, I believe you can see clearly this all was created out of Truth and Love. It is enormous and majestic.

There are many paths to choose from, the journey is uniquely vast. Choose the religious paths and you will find that its leaders have spread, in abundance, across the entire planet and have existed for thousands of years. Running their protection plan and ultimately, making this experience more fearful and stress-filled. However, the basis of religion started as something good, the idea was great, the path was a viable option to get access to the truth. But this was short lived due to the unfortunate character option-greed. The purpose of religion should have stayed to teach others that God exists, that Truth exists, and that we all need to live a compassionate and truthful life, simply trying to be a good person.

That truth is not found in material things but in the experience inside each of us. The wanting of material things produces greed. They believe that money has brought them this power and they continue to seek that power, sometimes ruthlessly. Because there is money needed to run a religion or a government, they have used fear and guilt to motivate people into paying for membership in a variety of creative ways. They perpetuate the existence of false truths with no real research into how one can realize their true eternal soul.

I am not saying that people who belong to a religion are lost but those who choose to allow the church to think for them and do not try to figure out who they are, will struggle to find enlightenment themselves. These are the ones who are most in jeopardy of becoming completely lost.

These people have fallen into the wrong pattern of thinking. They attend church yet judge others for not having the same religious beliefs. Religion isn't what makes someone a good person or not. Attendance at church isn't necessary to being a good person. These are the fallacies that are dominating the majority of the world.

Following the idea that going to church is the right thing to do and the only way to heaven, which is ultimately God, is an awfully simple way of experiencing the world. I believe with all of my being that humans were meant to transcend this place and return stronger, wiser, more knowledgeable beings.

I want to teach everyone I meet from this day forward to be truly happy here. It is not about when I get to heaven I will be happy or when I get this I will be happy. Be happy now. This is a very special place we get to live.

I believe this was supposed to be a beautiful paradise forever but this place has developed into a training world with good and evil jockeying for control. The greatest test of our eternal endurance will be how well we navigate throughout this experience over and over again.

I have often wondered: if God were to come here and command me to be happy, truly happy, every day, to learn everything about myself and enjoy my life, would I be able to do it?

Could He do it?

The choice to be happy is ours. No one controls that but the individual soul. It is based on the pattern of choices we make in our lives every single day…every single moment. Things may not go the way we want them to, but in each moment, we are presented with the choice to move in a new and improved direction.

There are wars being fought all over this world. Military and spiritual conflicts are waged with no real thought about the true worth of the soul. Men, women, and children are killed at a horrifying rate every single day. Spiritual leaders have for centuries charged man for consolation and relief, by forbidding the virtues that make existence possible, then attaching to mankind in order to collect donations for every soul, for as long as they can. I would think false damnation of the soul is the greatest sin of all. It appears that material greed is the driving force behind this sin. By being truly informed of the Truth, it is revealed that the material nature of this world is merely illusionary elements. Aspects of the eternal world. Very few get to realize this truth anymore.

This loss of the soul must stop somehow.

But how?

Who could stop something this old and developed that stretches to all parts of this world?

A training world is not meant to end in the destruction of the soul.

Why is this not realized by more?

What can I do to try and stop this?

He stopped writing and looked up at me; he appeared relieved, free from words that had been trapped in him for some time and now, as they needed to be, lay on those pages.

Smiling I asked, "Good writing?"

"I remember when we first met and you were telling me so much that my mind was spinning. You have always been so patient, kind, and understanding. You told me from early on: 'I want you to know that I am here to help you always.' You were flipping through some book. Was it this same book? I'm not really sure why I just remembered that but I recognize it as a truth that you will always be here to help me. You wrote this book, didn't you? You wrote this to help me understand?"

I got up and sat next to him on the rock.

"I will always be here to help you, Tristin. I wish I could just give you everything. I am almost certain you can handle it and things would be so much easier. But I remind myself to be patient because in actuality everything probably would not be okay if you were not ready and we just cannot take that chance. This is how it is for many. This is how parents feel about their children, if they could tell them, have them listen and understand they could save

204

them time. Naturally, at some point, we realize that it is not always about where we are headed but the collection of our experiences and our journey along the way. We do not have all that much time to explain everything. You have been here a while now."

I took a deep breath, then continued,

"This is a delicate process, with only one known effective way to use it. We do not want to push things too fast so that they are not truly learned. The book is a guide, it helps but I did not write it. However, I did help, at one point, put it together."

"I feel that I am ready to know what it is that I need to know," he said with such fire and certainty in his eyes. "I already have realized some important things necessary to continue in this process down the right path but I am certain that I can learn anything I will need to learn. If the knowledge is attainable, I will know it."

Opening the book, I flipped to a certain page and handed it to Tristin. "This is something that is extremely important and needs to be considered. It should help guide you in understanding a bigger piece of what it is you are dealing with."

Attempt to wrap your mind around the fact that I have existed for more than thirty billion years. I have learned so much, grown so much, and changed so much. Now I need to initiate change in an entire world that may not necessarily want to change. I must restore the necessary balance.

CHAPTER SIXTEEN

"Balance," Tristin said, getting up from the rock.

He walked around the clearing, touching the leaves on the trees and then kneeling as if to pray, dipped his hand in the cool water of the stream, the liquid flowing around his fingers.

"The yin and the yang, the right and the wrong, there really does need to be some bad to have good, right? Humans have to make bad decisions to realize that there was a better one they could have made. Isn't that how we grow?

"People are not perfect and are not always going to make the right choice but they need to *make it a high percentage of the time and they need to learn from their mistakes, in order to Become something more. This growth can lead to a balanced life. One must feel that life is worthwhile and understand that they can become something better than they are right now."*

Tristin laid himself down on the ground and let the sun radiate into him as if energizing his soul. I watched him for a moment. A wonderful feeling began flowing through me, I knew he was really here and recognizing who he was. He was not going to be lost here any longer, despite the initial family he had been given and the situations he had found himself in. I could see in his bright hazel-green eyes, he was not going to lose this battle. Picking up the book again, I rubbed the spine and felt the smoothness of it under my fingers. Running my fingers over the pages, I turned them again to a specific page that I had read and reread many times.
"Tristin," I said,

"Adonae wrote this on the day that he came to me and told me of his plan to come here. He gave me a book to hold onto until it was needed again.

Tristin sat up and took the book from my outstretched and patient hands, and began reading.

My dear Elizabeth,

I know that you will find this and understand.

The souls still claim to love me but they do not even know who I am. I am not what they have been taught, how do I show them so they will believe?

Things have not unfolded the way the stories tell it. The beginning is all wrong, so everything else has been so dreadfully wrong. I can change the dynamics of the current course of time by being born there as a human—my soul in a mortal body. I feel such an overwhelming sensation inside my core that I must go be there or more eternal damage will be done. I have tried every other possible way except taking on a physical form, in this way… birth.

Of course to fully realize who I am and reacquire all of the knowledge and power that I have obtained in my time will be difficult I know but I will do it, I promise you this, we will be reunited. I need to teach the world the Truth as a man.

I hope that you understand why I must do this. I need to help them understand that the imbalance of their reality is because of the necessity to have opposition in all things created. As I was creating perfection in parts of the universe, imperfection was being created as a by-product elsewhere. I did not understand this at first. Sebastian was the one to first bring it to my attention. Now I fully understand the reality of this.

This imperfection grew into the evil known in the world today...it has many forms. Eventually, it grew into living mortal beings continuing to recreate, taking up residence and feeding off of my paradise. Sebastian is my opposition now and the Truth behind the driving force of evil. His character is tainted by his lust for anger, hate, and control. He was easily blinded to many truths.

With all that I know to be true and eternal, I have determined that I do need to teach him the Truth, My way-what I know— something I should have done a long time ago. Now we have the possibility of two opposing forces becoming an imperfect union within the universe. Its existence will not be perfect but there will be a very clear choice to be made. I still believe that once fully understood, no one would choose wrongly. It is just that too much is hidden there.

I believe we can eliminate forever the evil…

I know I am the original cause of the birth of man from innocence. I feel it necessary to personally teach as many as I can; to save as many as I can from their false reality. I will be born into the world. I have deliberated this for a long, long time and I have decided to find out what kind of man I will become.

I love you so much and I will miss you. I have never really had to know what it is like to be without you...

Good bye for now...

I could feel Tristin watching me, trying to understand me. As he flipped forward one page in the book, he found a passage in a different handwriting than he had just read.

I knew the passage.

He did not.

My Adonae,

I knew that if I wrote you here, you would focus on what I feel I must say to you. I know the agony that you have been enduring for so long regarding your paradise. I see you weep for them all and I know that you feel responsible but you are not.

Someday I believe someone will be able to save them from themselves but you cannot decide to be born a mortal man.

You are Adonae-the master creator, the first one.

It is not your will that created what Sebastian has done with his power. His creations freely choose to create the reality that they live in. You made sure that they had the choice and that ability to freely choose is what can save them.

The beauty of this freedom is they choose to realize who they are. They cannot be forced to be good, to make good choices, or to be happy. This is the way that you felt was best and you are right, this is the way that is right, although not perfect.

I beg you, please do not go. Not because I am fearful that you will not return but simply and selfishly, I would miss you more than I could bear. I feel so torn about all of this, I know that you would not go unless you truly felt this was the right course of action to take and I trust you and your sense of judgment.

You are judgment.

You are Truth.

You are what is right and I love you and will continue to love you for all of eternity. Please hold on to this love and if you choose to go and

I cannot stop you, then I cannot promise I

will not follow you.

Either way...

my love...

I will see you soon.

CHAPTER SEVENTEEN

*Tristin looked up from the book, tears in the eyes.
"What is this?"*

*"I don't think that Adonae has ever read
that. She wrote it the day he left to come here."
"Is she here right now?" Tristin asked tentatively.
I shrugged. I wasn't certain. I had not begun
looking for her yet but I believe what she wrote.
We both sat there, lost in thought, as the sun
shrunk in the sky.*

"I think it's time you and I start back," I said to Tristin, bringing him back from wherever he was.

"Oh, yeah," he said, getting up and brushing off his jeans, the book in his right hand.

As if he could read my mind, he started to hand it to me. I shook my head and said, "It is yours."

His eyes lit up with excitement when he realized he could read the entire thing from front to back and not just passages and pieces. I am sure he will examine every word.

We started on our journey back, enjoying the coolness of the air as the sun slowly set behind the mountains.

After a few minutes of silence, I began talking again,

"I often consider myself a philosopher, a scientist, and a teacher but it is difficult to teach here because daily life is so misleading. Guiding a true and eternal being through this experience is a spectacular yet difficult adventure."

"Energy was realized to be everlasting. All things created to survive with energy, fade out of existence when their energy source dies but energy is eternally becoming something else. Accurate choices are the solution to the riddle; they are entertained by billions at random every day. These choices are the creators of tomorrow *in this world. People blame God for the way that their world is but they need to realize it is their 'creation-the state of disarray in their world. Even now, for you Tristin, you may only have a vague understanding of what is "real"; you are on the right path of total understanding. Try and know this:*

Adonae created the universe long, long before this planet was realized. He created all possible events, actions, and thoughts by making his first choice to realize that he already existed."
"Do you understand?"
"Yes," he said confidently.

"Do you know the theory about the fate of the universe that has all matter continuing to fly apart for billions of years and eventually time ending when everything is so far apart that there is nothing?
"Yeah"

"Well nothingness is how all things started, not how things will end. It doesn't ever end because Adonae exists."

"More than thirty billion years ago that nothingness was all that existed.

It was a mist of all potentiality,"

I was ripped from the book, startled by her contact, and feeling short of breath. She had grabbed my arm and squeezed. I felt that sense of surprise when you realize that you forgot where you are...shocking sometimes and this time was exceptional.

She was holding my right bicep; this caused me to turn my head toward her and my eyes straight to hers. It took a couple of seconds before I was able to focus on her words, "We are boarding now."

Wow... you are beautiful is all I wanted to say but I only was able to manage a mumbled,
"Oh...thank you very much."
I got to my feet in unison with her and gathered my Self, my bag and the book. Trailing right behind her to the end of the 'Now Boarding' line, I pulled my business card out of my pocket, the one I had found in the book, and quickly thrust it into the book's thick pages.
As the line started flowing forward, I tapped her on the shoulder with the book. She turned toward me and I handed it to her.
"Here you go. I think you will enjoy it."
"So, you finished?

"Yeah, kind of, I think I might have missed a few pages, but the book is great. You should check it out and let me know what you think."

"Cool, thank you. I didn't have anything to read for the flight. Give me your address and I will send it back to you."

"No, no...it's not mine to claim. I found it here and want to give it to you- it's pretty deep...uniquely interesting, let me know what you think"

"Wow, thanks, that's really sweet of you," she smiled.

I smiled back and informed her,

"I put my card in the book- in case you ever want to discuss the book over coffee or something, you can give me a call. It is definitely a book that we could have many conversations over."

With the most perfectly compassionate grin that I had ever seen, she said-

"Absolutely... thank you, I love books and I love coffee."

She smiled at me again and I returned the favor, then we both turned to board the plane.

CHAPTER EIGHTEEN

What a nice guy, he did seem strangely familiar, his eyes…so intense.

I found my seat, 23C, and sat down. Buckling my seatbelt, I opened the book to where his card was.

It has been a long time since someone had given me a book I thought.

I scanned over the page where he had left his card but my attention quickly returned to him and the business card that lay in my hand...his business card. It read:

Hybris

The other side of the card, on the bottom, gave me his number

Alex Walker
623-555-8925

I was certain I would call him.

Looking away from the card, I turned my attention back to the book in my lap and began to read.

In this life, you will find it far more useful and enjoyable if you choose to understand the paradigm.

Don't just be content to exist.

Make discoveries on how you are going to provide for your life and live this experience. There is no time to worry about how you are going to leave this experience.

Live life where you are happy every day. When you really, truly realize and try the possibility, it makes sense to you and it comes easily. There is a full realization point; an epiphany must occur. Know that you can be happy, creative, and energetic.

You don't have to necessarily experience bad things, although sometimes they might happen to you. You can't fully understand it until you realize it in your soul. It takes a leap of faith not only believing but to know something deep in your soul.

You chose to be here.

Remember that.

It is initially overwhelming on your body and mind, the whole thing is surreal. It is not something that you see and go to. You are it. It is your Truth. You must realize it inside of you.

Live life by the guidelines I am giving you and you will find the Truth. The Truth is beyond the basic understanding levels. You cannot find it on autopilot.

Once realized, it will be amazing for you to understand that the whole universe is a giant system. Break each and every moment down, progressively and completely, all along the way. Mindfully navigate your path, it allows you to really see the system and how it works. Your family, your job, your friends are forms of systems and this method will allow you to eventually become consistently perfect.

Once you understand that it is a system, it becomes something you can work with and improve upon. There are some levels that are more challenging and others that are optimal. Always seek out optimum levels. Look at the areas you can make big impacts in and learn to improve every level your system is operating on constantly.

It is something that requires you to study the forest from above the forest as well as from within the forest. The work done from above is very revealing as to how the forest works. You are a part of a great system and you can create the ability for yourself to be truly at peace every day and achieve everything you want by constantly working, setting goals and achieving those goals.

Don't get lazy, stay consistent!

Existing physically is exhilarating and challenging, sometimes the possibility of tragedy exists. The tragic part of the experience is viewed differently in the eternal world. Tragic markers can be signs, red flags that you are heading in the wrong direction in one or more areas.

Be honest in all of your actions.

Remember always to research intensely to know the areas most in need of improvement.

And to think of how lucky a being I am to look at your soul and know all.

Love is not expressed in words alone.
Love is eternal.

To find that one being that completes who we are becoming and to create life in a way that is real and true.

There is a struggle going on all around, completely hidden from the atmosphere of everyday life.

Language controls it.

Be aware and utilize all of your senses.

This is a piece of what you can know and experience.
Imagine the ability to ask someone a question and see their thought processes unfolding as they form their answers and then put them in to words.

Imagine the ability to stop time.

Many, many powerful tricks exist.

Discover why the simple concept of the power of the four foundations: choice, patience, love, and balance exists. Without these four, people are confused and lost, searching the world for something. Language distorts everything because it has limits to what it can explain on the human level. Reality is not what you think or write that it is.

It is what it is...eternally.

Only thing I could do was wise up
See the whole picture and
Change what I could.

I saw Sebastian the other day from a distance, he didn't see me. It's not like he would have even recognized me without looking me in the eye.

It is an odd feeling to see someone you have known so long from a distance, watching them operate. I do not have ill feelings toward Sebastian anymore for what he has allowed himself to become but I am still extremely disappointed with him. He has had so many years on this Earth to figure it out. I cannot agree with Sebastian because he is wrong.

His vision of this world is false and evil and can never be allowed to exist in eternity. Sebastian is angry at the realization of his own fall but his fall was the working of his own self-fulfilling prophecies from within the paradise.

Jon has commented that he believes I will someday forgive Sebastian for his ignorant and false divine drive. If Sebastian were to help clean up the mess he has created, I could consider it but he is not.

I do not believe it is about my forgiveness as much as it is about Sebastian forgiving himself and his fellow lost gods forgiving him. However, that process has to start with Sebastian admitting that he was and is wrong.

The pseudo-truth of this reality is that Sebastian is controlling as many minds as he can, simply by controlling the flow of everyday life.

People choose if they want the correct way or the false path. Sebastian chose to communicate through the surroundings of the soul mind in order to create what his version of the Truth is, instead of allowing them to learn and realize who they truly, naturally and eternally are, then watch them naturally select the truth.

I learned long ago and have always known that the only correct way to become enlightened and accurate was to realize Yourself out of the dream.

Help is beneficial when it is planted firmly in the truth. Then it can then guide you in the proper direction.

But people have become lost in a currently created mind set, and no gods have come out of the mist for hundreds of years now.

Sebastian is completely unaware that I, long ago, was born onto this Earth. If he were aware, he would be spending his time searching for me.

I was born into this life, just as every baby is born; innocent, pure and empty because I chose to solve the greatest riddle ever developed.

Initially, I was an unknowing being that had to realize my own potential, my characteristics and my truth. This was not easy; it required great patience and the ability to enjoy and record the experiences along the way.

I learned how to pass them along.

There are some things that you just know.
Why?
How?

Unlocking the mind is a complicated process.
Figuring it all out,
Simply by
Honestly and consistently **TRYING**.

Beginning to understand
I am not perfect.
but
I'm becoming more.

"Miss"

I was brought back to the present, forgetting for a second where I was-

Is this really happening, dashed through my mind.

"Excuse me, Miss, would you care for something to drink?" the flight attendant asked me.

"Ummm? Yes please- I will have a ginger ale, thank you," I said, looking up at her and smiling kindly. I could feel my face heating up with embarrassment for being so wrapped up in my reading that I didn't hear her.

"All right," she said and began the process of getting my drink.

I noticed that she even seemed awkward and somewhat new at what she does.

"Here you go," she said, as she handed me the drink.

"Thank you very much," I replied back, taking a sip. She smiled and nodded and continued on her way down the aisle.

I took another sip and then looked down quickly, remembering the book lying in my lap.

Yum......good soda, my mouth was drier than I realized.
Thinking about what I was reading, I pondered,
I wonder what I am Becoming?

Curiously I flipped to the next page which was the second to the last page in the book... and was surprised and slightly confused to read the words on the last page-

You must learn quicker this time-

You are not who you think you are!

You are Adonae!

And we desperately need for you to realize yourself out of this mist and help us!

My life paused but my mind was racing.

What if...?

I flipped to the cover, stroked the leather and read aloud the title-

...a story about god

What if this is real?

That would be amazing!

I turned the last page and found twelve words at the bottom:

Everything in this book could be false.

But what if it's not?